MANDIBLE

IAN WOODHEAD

SEVERED PRESS
HOBART TASMANIA

MANDIBLE

Copyright © 2019 Ian Woodhead

WWW.SEVEREDPRESS.COM

ISBN: 978-1-925840-66-7

CHAPTER ONE
THE FIRST WARNING

The moment that Ellis Patterson set foot in the Bombay Diner, her shoulders, laden with the stress of what had happened that morning, just floated away. She believed that the tantalising scent of hot tandoori spice-coated chicken breast, coupled with the strong smell emanating from the ever present rotating donner kebab spit might have something to do with it. That beaming smile belonging to Aroon Khan, the owner's only son probably helped a little.

"And suddenly, the whole world has become a joy to behold!"

"Hi, Aroon," she replied. "Just the whole world?" For the first time since the dining room incident, that morning, Ellis felt her lips moving in an upwards direction. If did feel good to smile, even if it was solely because this idiot was trying it on with her, as per usual.

"If you want more than the world, lovely lady, then you are going to have to work for it!" He leaned over the counter. "How about a quick kiss? You know, just to seal the marriage proposal that I'm someday going to give you."

"I'll have two onion bhajiis, a couple of chicken pakoras and a portion of chips."

"My dad's framing the doorway, isn't he?"

She gave him a single but sly nod.

"That'll be four fifty please."

Ellis paid with her phone, so doing her best not to giggle. Mr Romeo had almost been caught yet again. His dad had warned him a couple of times not to try it on with the female customers. She made her way to her usual table, grateful to see that the greasy black haired teen previously occupying it when she walked in, had already gone.

She sat down, making sure not to choose the bright red, hard plastic seat which greaseball had used. As Aroon was doing his best to look professional while he prepared her food under the watchful eye of his father, she decided to observe the local wildlife instead. Ellis casually tapped her fingers against the table surface while listening to two elderly women comment over the lack of places in the market where you could get a decent cup of tea any more.

Ellis hadn't asked for a drink. She hated tea but she'd need a coke after scoffing all that spicy food, that's for sure. That could wait. There was a stall in the market, just three rows up where they sold three cans for a quid. That would do her. The other two would go in her backpack for later on.

For a Saturday lunchtime, the largest market in Bradfield was packed out. Normally, this place wasn't that busy, even on a weekend. Thanks to the new shopping centre, they had built at the bottom of the city centre last year, the market trade had lessened considerably. Why travel all the way up Darlygate to reach some market that should have been demolished years ago when you can go into the new mall, right next to the bus and train terminal? The new shopping mall even had a Taco Bell!

Unlike most teenagers her age, Ellis didn't care for the overpriced clothing shops, bland food outlets and the shops packed with overpriced pointless junk. She preferred her shopping experience to be on a more personal level. As well as a lot sodding cheaper.

Those two old ladies had wandered off. She wished them good luck in finding a café in here which served decent tea. She knew why it seemed half the city was in here today. Hell, everybody knew. The council had closed most of the bottom part of town because of the recent bout of mini earthquakes. Ellis idly traced her finger through a coke juice puddle while watching Aroon approach her table. The smile had left his mouth but those lovely, large brown eyes still retained that cheeky sparkle.

Earthquakes in Bradfield, how weird was that? How on earth could some crappy city in the north of England possibly suffer from a series of earthquakes? It sounded too ridiculous to be true but they had happened. During the last tremor which caused the council and the authorities to finally take some action, no matter how pointless, some poor mother lost her pushchair and her six month old son into a deep crevice which opened up right under her feet. A bunch of burly firemen had been able to pull the kid to safety but the resulting TV exposure had made certain people, high up, try to do something about it.

"There you go, enjoy your meal." He placed the food on the pale blue, plastic counter and turned around.

"Aroon," she glanced over at the counter and saw his father serving a couple of Asian girls. It didn't surprise her to see those two old ladies were back, standing outside and studying the menu. "Do you think you could fetch a cloth? That dirty sod before me spilled his drink all over the table, it's a right mess."

He grinned. "Sure, won't be a mo."

She took a bite from one of the pakoras and watched another couple of kids join the queue. She was sure that Aroon's dad would be glad of the custom but she wasn't too keen. Ellis came here specifically because at this time, she normally had the place to herself. She also would have preferred to spend a bit more time letting Aroon chat her up and after today, Ellis needed all the buttering up she could get.

It looked like the two old ladies weren't interested in the goodies they had to offer in here after all. Aroon came back, his right hand holding a yellow cloth. She moved over to the wall while he briskly cleaned up the spilled coke. "Are you okay, Aroon? You don't seem your usual self."

He shrugged. "Oh, you know, the usual family bullshit, nothing much different."

"You mean your dad still isn't too keen on you opening your own restaurant?" The brief glimpse of pain she saw across his features told her she'd hit the jackpot.

"Yeah. He still doesn't think I'm old enough. Do you know what he said to me last night? He told me that if I had any hopes of opening my own business, I needed to go work with my cousin in his take-away in Burnley for a few months, just to find out exactly what hard work really is." Aroon quickly looked up. "Like I don't know what hard work is? I practically do everything in here while he sits in the back, playing stupid games on his phone and drinking mango lassi." He took a deep breath. "Sorry, that was uncalled for. Look, Dad is off to the cash and carry in a few minutes. Eat your food nice and slow, okay?" He pushed the cloth into his back pocket. "There you go, madam. Your table is clean again. It couldn't be cleaner if I had used my own tears." Aroon smiled softly. "Tears I lose nightly due to you continuing to deny our love."

"Seriously," she said, chuckling. "Go on, bugger off with you!" Ellis waited for him to get back around the counter and start to serve the group of kids before returning to her food. She picked up one of the bhajis and took a large bite, while watching one the those kids, a ginger-haired boy, a couple of years younger than her, take out his phone and start frantically jabbing his finger against the screen. Judging from his expression, it looked like the kid had thought his whole world had come to an end. Knowing the generation coming up behind her, that could be anything from someone on his Facebook list lagging off his last post or someone sending him a doctored Snapchat photo of his mum.

Ellis took her eyes off the kid's traumatised expression as it was depressing the hell out of her. Right now, she needed goodness in her life. The only thing which came even close to supplying a much-needed injection of happiness was the food in front of her. The chips helped to offset the tongue-tingling sensation caused by the spicy snacks. Ellis found the right ratio of three chips to every bite of bhaji or pakora, while allowing herself to zone out to avoid dwelling on the incident involving her mum and dad a few hours ago.

One of the kids cried out while simultaneously discovering her table vibrating. It wasn't just the table. The chairs were moving too. One of the lads grabbed the edge of the counter while his mate, the ginger kid, held his phone up in the air. Christ on a bike, he was filming it! As quickly as it started, the tremors stopped. She looked down to find one of her bhajis had fallen on the floor. "Just marvellous," she muttered.

Both Aroon and his dad had run out from behind the counter, picking up fallen chairs, reassuring their customers as well as doing their hardest to laugh it off. They weren't the only ones in the diner who were trying to see the funny side of it. Ellis heard one of the lads tell the ginger kid that the milkman was asking his mum right now if the earth moved for her. This crap insult earned the other kid a punch in the shoulder.

Two more customers rushed out, a young woman and a middle-aged man, both with their phones glued to their ears. She had no intention of leaving, not until she ate the rest of her food. Ellis picked up a couple more chips. She paused, saw the kids run off while Aroon's dad rushed into the back.

"Aroon," she said, standing up. "Where's everybody going?"

He shrugged. "No idea, Ellis," he replied. The young man turned and looked at the door leading to the back room for a few seconds before joining her. He sat opposite the girl. "We had one like that yesterday. A bit longer too. Nobody left then. They'll be back, don't you worry about it. Now," he leaned forward and rested his elbows on the table. "What's wrong, I haven't seen you looking so glum for years. The last time was, let me think." He smiled. "That's it! When Mr Ward caught Andrew Davis with his tongue down your neck in the middle of Biology."

"I can't believe you still remember that, Aroon."

"Well, who can blame a man for being jealous? He had the ultimate privilege of caressing your silken skin, he gazed into the eyes which belong inside the face of some mystical Goddess."

"I swear down, if you don't cut it out, I'll shove these chips up your nose!"

"Sorry," he replied. "Sometimes, I tend to get a bit carried away."

"Just sometimes? You do know that if Jason heard you talking like that to me, he'd do more than push cold chips up your nose."

"He's not the one who's upset you?"

Ellis shook her head. Things with her and Jason were going great. For the first time in the twenty-four years she'd been on this planet, Ellis had found someone who, she believed, truly loved her. It was going so great that last night, Jason just happened to mention what she thought about getting a place together. That's where the trouble started. Not with Jason, but with her adopted parents, when Ellis broke the news to them at breakfast.

"Would Jason really try to insert chips up my nose?"

"If he found out about you chatting me up every time I came in here, he'd push the kebab spit up there." Ellis chuckled. "Just kidding, he probably wouldn't even care." Jason knew all about Aroon's rather over-familiar behaviour and thought it kinda sweet, suggesting that he probably had a crush on her back when they went to school and believes his Romeo act is his way of working it out of his system.

"Just be thankful that I didn't try to hang on to Andrew Davis."

Aroon looked down at the table. "Yeah, let us thank Allah for him saving you from a fate worse than death."

"Thanks Aroon, but I don't think Allah had much to do with it. The guy was a dick and got what he deserved." Their town's resident bad boy might have been a looker back when they were all fifteen, but even then, the lad had already started hanging out with the wrong crowd. The wrong crowd which helped to put him inside for almost a dozen aggravated assault charges.

As for the nuclear explosion which occurred across the table, she decided to keep that to herself for the moment. Besides, Ellis noticed the back door opening, it looked like his parental problem had made another appearance. She stood up. "Aroon, I really have to go. Jason's supposed to be meeting me. Don't worry about me, honey. I'll be fine." She caught the disapproving stare coming from Aroon's dad. Ellis winked then leaned across the table and kissed the tip of his nose. "We couldn't stuff chips up your nose, Aroon, it's way too pretty for that!"

Ellis left the diner, and stepped back into the market causeway. The thought of how much trouble her actions might have caused Aroon vanished when she found herself alone. There wasn't anybody around. It was as if she walked into the diner on a busy Saturday morning, and walked out twenty-four hours later when the place was closed.

"What the hell?" Ellis spun around hoping that perhaps her friend and his dad might have some answer but they had gone too. The temptation to shout if anyone was around almost overcame her. Instead, Ellis jogged down the deserted causeway, heading straight for the meat and fish quarter, where Jason was meeting up with her. She'd feel a lot better then. Her boyfriend was bound to know what had happened here.

CHAPTER TWO
AN EASY BLAG

The phrase taking candy from a baby ran through his mind, over and over. The man sat to the left of Andrew Davis would not shut the fuck up. He kept asking him something and even his hastily assembled mantra didn't help to zone out that annoying whine. "What's that?" he asked. His voice sounded as mild as ever, despite knowing that his already short temper had already blown a fuse.

"It's your turn, Davis. Are you going to play or what?"

"Like taking candy from a baby," he whispered before throwing down a royal flush. "There you go, you fucker. That's how you do it!" He glared at the old bastard, silently daring the bastard to accuse Davis of cheating.

Nelson Bradshaw threw his cards down in disgust. "Cheeky twat, I'm not that much of a crap player."

"I was talking about the blag."

"Oh right. Fair enough, I'll let you off then. Want me to deal 'em out?"

Andrew picked up the dealt cards. Their next job would be as easy as beating this idiot. He threw down two cards and glanced across at the only source of light in this dank and dismal flat. Their target lay just across the road. The local branch of Bradfield's Black Lotus Bank, wouldn't know what hit them when the three of them raided it in a few hours' time. Andrew took the offered cards, raised the stake by throwing his mum's necklace into the pot and impatiently waited for the old bastard to shock him rigid with whatever crap he held in those effeminate, slender hands.

Nelson could have been a piano player. Davis thanked God that the foul-mouthed shithead, who usually stunk of over-boiled cabbage, chose a criminal occupation. Thanks to a bit of bribery and the actions of a fellow prisoner who took an instant dislike to Nelson, Andrew now had the best safe cracker in the north of England in the palm of his hands.

Speaking of hands, Nelson threw down a couple of pairs. Andrew resisted the urge to gloat before dropping three queens. "Had enough, old man?" He picked up the deck and gave them a quick shuffle.

"I can't do this without a hot drink."

Nelson switched his attention to the remaining member of their little group, Tony Wright. He hadn't joined in with the card game on account that he said he didn't know how to play, so while Andrew won twenty quid, a gold watch and a go with Nelson's daughter, that clown spent the time gazing out of the window.

"Oi, make yourself useful and get your arse in that kitchen. We're both dying for a brew."

"No can do, Nelson," he replied, not turning around. "There's no milk left."

Andrew eased himself up. He pulled out a pound coin from his back pocket then sauntered over to the window. The kid must have sensed his approach but before he could turn around, Andrew grabbed the back of his head and pushed it hard against the glass. "It was your job to make sure we didn't run out of essential supplies. Do you not remember me saying those sweet words to you?"

"Sorry, Guv. I kinda forgot."

Andrew heard oodles of resentment and defiance in those five little words and wondered how much punishment this kid would be able to take before he smacked all that attitude out of him and as tempting as it was to show the kid that he was now playing in the big boy's league, time was against him. "Best pop to the shops then, sonny. Here's a quid. Don't take too long." Andrew grabbed the boy's little finger and bent it back. He didn't ease the pressure until the lad cried out. "I expect some change back." Andrew walked back to the only chair in the room and slumped into it. He idly picked at the loose red fabric on the chair arm before picking up the cards. "Do you fancy one more game while we wait for the idiot to come back?"

"No, I'm bored with you cheating." Nelson leaned over the upturned milk-crate which served as their table. "He's going to turn on you one day, Andy. Tony ain't too keen on anyone threatening him."

"He won't turn, Nelson. The brat looks up to me. It's as plain as day."

"Don't bet on that, you're not that enigmatic." Nelson walked over to the window. "He's just set off. How much are you betting he comes back with a can of beer?"

"You haven't got anything left to bet with, Nelson. Look, do me a favour will you?"

"What's that?"

"Shut your hole. I'm trying to think."

Worrying about the kid's attitude would get him nowhere. He knew Nelson was right about not pushing the boy too hard. It's just that Andrew couldn't help himself. Whenever he sensed anyone trying it on, his temper just flared up. He couldn't control it.

The old man walked right past him. "I'm going for a piss. Give those cards a good shuffle, I want my stuff back."

Andrew waited for him to leave the room. He left the cards on the crate and walked back over to the window, parted the filthy net curtains and gazed onto the gloomy street. Common sense advised him to call this thing off, that doing a job in his home town only a week after they'd released him was just asking for trouble.

That much was true. The bizzies would be knocking on his door hours after they'd cleaned out that bank. Of course they would, he'd be their prime suspect. Thing is, if some other set of cockwombles turned over a local bank, they'd still be knocking on his door, so what did he have to lose? Kinda made sense that he should get in first before some other outfit saw how shoddy their security was.

Common sense was subjective anyhow, everybody knew that. He spotted movement down below. The shop door opened and the boy left the shop. He nodded in approval when he spotted the carton of milk in his left hand although he wasn't that impressed when he noticed the chocolate bar sticking out of the kid's back trouser pocket. He told his temper to calm the fuck down.

Tony stopped by the side of the road and waited for a bus to trundle past. Andrew felt the shaking up here. He suddenly grabbed the side of the window. It wasn't the bus causing that! Andrew ran over to his chair and threw himself in it, grabbed the sides and clenched his teeth while waiting for it to stop. He so wanted to close his eyes but that had only made the sensation even worse the last time this happened a couple of days ago.

"Jesus Fucking Christ!" he moaned.

The shakes continued for another couple of seconds before diminishing. Andrew wiped his forehead, clamped down on the urge to vomit and did his best to contain the utter terror which still ran riot around his body.

"That was a good one. Better than a roller-coaster, they are," said Nelson, walking past his chair. "Quite strong, maybe even the strongest so far." He sat down in his spot. "I hope you've given those cards a good shuffle."

Andrew managed a brief nod.

"Oh yeah? Well, I hope you don't mind me double checking, you know, just to be totally sure." He picked up the cards and started to shuffle them. "Tony's back, by the way. He got in seconds before the tremors started. Looks like you were right, by the way. He did come back with the milk."

Those tremors terrified him. In fact, they did more than just that.

Andrew had known terror. In the first few months inside, him and terror became the best of friends, almost intimate lovers, thanks to a certain warden who was best pals with the uncle of one of the lads who Andrew hospitalised. The warden didn't do anything to him. Mr Ward wasn't that dumb. Instead, he made sure that Andrew ended up sharing a cell with Harry Johnstone, the local psycho. Harry had family outside who needed looking after and Mr Ward was only too happy to send anonymous money packages to his family in return for a few favours. Harry didn't mind. He liked working with his hands.

The shaking and vibrations caused by whatever the hell it was under the earth sent Andrew's body into an almost complete shutdown. He remembered his mum having a phobia of spiders and as stupid as it sounded, her reaction when she spotted some little brown eight-legged beast in the bathroom was exactly how he felt. Was it even possible to have an earthquake phobia?

Tony entered the room, slopped two teas on the floor beside the two men and went back to his place by the window. He didn't bother looking out, instead, he slid down to the floor, leant against the wall and dug out his phone. Two seconds later, the boy's thumbs were dancing across the glass. That would be him quiet for the next few hours then. Tony loved his phone games. In fact, it seemed to be the only thing that made him use more than his usual emotion of miserable bastard.

What would he do if there was another tremor right in the middle of doing the job? He'd be fucked. Hell, they all would, meaning he'd end up back in HMP Fulton and back under the watchful eye of Mr. Ward. Shit, that could not happen.

"Are you going to play your hand, Andrew?" Nelson smiled, showing him his blackened teeth. "You could fold, if you like. I'm cool with that. As long as you agree to give back everything you stole from me."

"Like that is ever going to happen. And, for your information, you old fucker, I stole nothing. It was all won fair and square. Ain't my fault that you're crap." He picked the cards from the table, threw away two and glanced at his watch. They had one more hour to kill before they needed to move. Now that he'd recovered, he fully intended to clean Nelson out. After that, Andrew wanted to persuade the miserable bastard standing by the window to join in. He wasn't an idiot. Tony did know how to play. The kid learnt inside, from him, when something just terrible happened to poor Harry Johnstone and this new kid ended up being his cellmate for his last remaining six months, until the parole board decided that, in their wisdom, this poor reformed ex-bank robber was no longer a threat to the public.

Andrew received a pair of nines. If his luck continued to hold, that crappy phone of Tony's would belong to him before the hour was up. "Okay then, Nelson, let's see what you are holding." He threw the twenty quid that he took from the old man a while back, into the pot. "Or you can fold, if you like. I'm cool with that too."

CHAPTER THREE
A QUESTION ANSWERED

She felt like such a bloody idiot when she ran over to the nearest stall and leaned over the counter, to discover the holder on his hands and knees. He looked up and blinked a couple of times before kneeling up. "Are you okay there, love?" he asked.

Ellis nervously smiled at the young man before shaking her head. "No, I'm fine. Sorry." She beat a hasty backwards retreat while spotting the heads popping up past the counters of a jeweller's stall and a comic book stand. Jason and her had even talked about the council posters which went up around the city a couple of days ago, advising all members of the public to go down on their hands and knees in the event of another tremor to avoid falling over. It also mentioned getting away from any buildings too. She guessed the stall holders believed that didn't apply to them.

Halfway towards the meat and fish quarter, Ellis spotted a familiar and very welcome young man frantically waving at her. When she didn't immediately respond, he climbed on top of one of the children's rides and waved even harder. That soon stopped when the two old women she saw earlier stood in front of the ride. Ellis giggled at the sight of those two frail women giving her boyfriend a piece of their mind. She leaned against the side of a handbag stall with her arms folded and waited for them to finish.

"You could have saved me from their harshness, young lady," said Jason, a moment later after managing to get away from the women.

"I'm a little shocked that you didn't get their number. You've always said that you wanted a foursome."

"Wait, did you really say that or am I in the wrong reality again?"

"Hush up, Jay. You love all the attention. It turns you on." She took his hand while watching the two women vanish into a café next to the Black Lotus bank. She hoped they found their magical tea in there, it might help them calm down. "Now that you've finished chatting up a couple of mature ladies, perhaps you'll now tell me why you had to see me during my lunch break?"

He nodded. "How long do you have left before the workhouse beckons?"

"I took my full hour and spent twenty minutes of that grabbing food and shoving it down my neck. I'll let you do the maths."

"Right, so what? You have a couple of minutes left?" He grinned and gave her hand a tight squeeze. "Come on, young lady. This is going to slay you!" Jason led her through the large covered market, walking past stalls selling everything from second-hand goods to genuine Indian antiques. This place had everything and anything. Except for, perhaps, a shop which sold a decent cup of tea. Oh, and designer shops, big name brand outlets, and all the usual chain-store places. For all that stuff, the average Bradfield shopper went to the new mall. Until the council closed it down.

Now that the tremor had gone, the market began to fill up again, making it increasingly difficult to get anywhere fast. It made progress harder, due to Jason taking her straight to the area where most of the youngsters hung out.

He pulled her past the large retro arcade hall, the mini cinema and the row of ethnic take-out stalls before stopping in front of the single empty stall in this sector. "There you go, what do you think, Ellis?"

"Think of what?" She gave the decrepit old shack a single cursory glance then looked past the eyesore and spotted a stall selling Polish food. That wasn't here the last time she walked around the market. It didn't look all that busy and...

Ellis spun around when the penny finally dropped. "No, no way, Jason. Please tell me that you're not thinking about renting this broken down old thing, that this is another one of your dumb jokes." She didn't need his affirmation to know that he wasn't having her on.

"We talked about this, Ellis." He tried to grab her hand but she pulled it back. "Hell, I seem to recall you were all for me starting my own business."

"For crying out loud. I didn't mean this. I thought you were thinking carrying on working with your dad but branching out and doing a few jobs on the side, you know, creating your own set of contacts and building a reputation before starting out on your own."

He sighed. "You really don't listen. Ellis, how many times have I told you how much I hate being a sparky? The last thing I want to do is to follow in my dad's footsteps."

"But the money is good, Jason. Plus, you're really good at it. Why change?"

"Do you want a list?"

She finally took his hand. "Jason, what I want is for us to be together, to have our own place and be happy."

"Well then, there you go!" he announced. "We're both on the same wavelength. Ellis, look. I know that it's a bit rundown right now but it'll fix up. Plus, it'll cost next to nothing to sort out. Those contacts you just mentioned. I have plenty of those. I could get this stall looking far better than all the others on this row and all it'll cost me is a few quid and a round or two down at the Hope and Anchor."

Ellis forced herself to look at the damned hut again. "What exactly are you intending to sell in your brightly painted hut?" She waited for his reply. When he failed to respond, her heart sank even lower. Ellis turned into the biggest grin she'd ever seen. He looked like some kid who'd just won a toy shop in the Lottery. Which, she guessed, probably wasn't that far from the truth.

Three years separated her and Jason Langley, but sometimes it felt like a lifetime. Her boyfriend had achieved more in his life than she could ever imagine. Jason had visited most of the continents before he reached his teenage years, thanks to his father's previous job. At the age of eighteen, he joined the army and in those five years of service, he faced combat in two arenas.

Yet, she knew none of this when they first got together, a few months ago. All Ellis knew back at that party her mate dragged her to, was she really wanted to get to know the over excitable young man who was currently dancing on the dinner table with a colander on his head while juggling four eggs when she arrived.

They had hit it off almost immediately. Perhaps it was the child-like innocence she saw in those big blue eyes that attracted her to him or that ability he possessed to make everyone around him feel so at ease? Even her pretend parents approved of her latest catch, that alone had to be a first. Jason even got on with her pretend father, so much so that the old man even took him up into the loft to show off his model railway layout.

She should have known right at that point, from the way Jason's eyes lit up at the sight of all those scale model locomotives, that her boyfriend and her pretend dad shared something in common. Jason was a toy collector. This little factoid presented itself when he finally brought her home to meet his lovely parents and he used this opportunity to show her his own man cave, only his room looked like he'd just cleaned out half a dozen toy shops. He sat her down and showed her his Hot Wheels collection, his thirty year old Transformers before he allowed her to gaze upon his Lego mini-figures.

Ellis now understood why she saw the eyes of a child fixed into that beautifully shaped head.

"You are thinking of selling toys?"

He nodded. "Obviously. What else would I sell? Look, I'm not talking about all that other cheapo, knock off crap that all the other toy stalls in here sell and not the overpriced rubbish that the two shops in the new mall sell either. I'm going to fill this stall with toys from yesteryear to appeal to the customers with oodles of cash and with that far off glint of nostalgia in their eyes. To the parents who cannot understand why their kids want them to hand over a tenner for some brightly coloured plastic egg which contains a shitty little doll which probably costs 20p to make." He glided his fingers down the wooden wall. "I want to give them back a piece of their childhood that they thought they lost."

"You mean you want to sell stuff to people just like my pretend dad."

He nodded again. "Absolutely, this city is full of people just like him, Ellis."

"I fucking hope not," she muttered.

"You don't approve?"

She didn't need to look at his face to know she'd just ripped out his heart. The underlying tone was right there in those words. It took a great deal of effort not to start yelling. God, that naïve optimistic streak of his could really get on her tits. Ellis noticed the vendor from the next stall was beginning to take an interest. "Please, don't come over here," she whispered. Having an audience would only make him worse.

Ellis turned. "It's the risk, Jason. That's what I'm concerned about. What if it fails? Right now, we need a bit of stability in our lives. Especially if we are going to live together."

"So, it's a risk. Living your life is a risk." He took both her hands. "Ellis, listen to me. We only have one shot at life, and if my rather brief experience of it has taught me anything, it's that if you see an opportunity, then reach out with both hands and reel that sucker in!" Jason wrapped his hands around her back and gave Ellis a gentle squeeze. "This will work, I guarantee it."

"You don't know the first thing about operating a market stall."

"So what? I didn't know how to fire a weapon until they showed me. I didn't know anything about being an electrician a few years ago. I didn't even know how to wire a plug. Don't worry about it. I can learn." He released one arm and used it to wave at the vendor next to them. "Hi there, how are you doing?" he shouted.

Ellis pulled him away, groaning silently. "I need to get back to work. They're in the middle of a big order and are watching us, making sure that we're not taking the piss with their break times."

"It's like being back at school, Ellis. Do you think you'll get detention if you're late?" He waved at the vendor again before leading her away from the empty stall. "I wouldn't give you detention, my love. I might smack your bum a couple of times though." He chuckled. "But only if you smack mine after."

She stopped walking. "You're really serious about this?"

"Totally. I really do want you to smack my bum."

"How about I punch you in the face instead? Christ, will you quit it with the fooling about?" Ellis knew she was close to tears.

Jason abruptly dragged her towards the retro arcade and sat her down on the wooden bench outside. "You told them, didn't you? I mean about us finding a place."

She nodded. "How did you know that?"

"It was on the front page of the Daily Mail this morning. How do you think I knew? I take it they weren't too happy about it?"

"What do you think?" Ellis couldn't hold them back. Tears streamed down her cheeks. "I don't get it. What is wrong with them? I thought they liked you, Jason. It's just not fair."

"It wouldn't have made any difference if you walked in one day with some spotty, foul-mouthed druggie and announced that you and Malcolm were emigrating to China. The reaction would have been the same."

"Malcolm?"

He grinned. "Why not? I knew a lad in Afghanistan called Malcolm who wasn't impartial to a bit of powder. Look, never mind all that. The point still stands, Ellis. It's not me and it isn't you either. Taking you on was the biggest risk that your adoptive parents ever undertook. Most people really don't like change, they embrace the familiarity. There's nothing wrong with that, it's just how we're built. They were young when they adopted you."

"Not that young."

"They were both in their late thirties, Ellis. That's still young, and twenty-four years later, that familiarity has grown from a groove into a deep, steep-sided valley. They can't face the thought of you not being around."

"You have got to be shitting me, Jason. They both can't stand me."

"That's bollocks, and you know it. They love you very much."

"Yeah, right. They have a funny way of showing it." She stood up. "I've got to go. I'm going to be late."

He pulled her back down. "Listen to me, Ellis. When your dad found you, covered in blood, he honestly thought you were dead, that they had killed you. Just as the intruders killed your real parents."

Ellis went white. "How did you know that?"

"They brought you up as their own, Ellis. Cared for you, protected you and gave you everything you wanted. Including love."

She was still reeling from what he'd just said. Her pretend parents had always been open and frank with how she came to be in their care but nobody else knew. They moved to Bradfield a few months after the incident. Nobody here knew who she was. "Jason, how did you find out? My pretend parents wouldn't tell you, that's for sure."

"I'm a man of many talents, as well you know, my darling." He stood up and pulled Ellis to her feet. "I promise I'll tell you tonight. Right now, I need to get you back to work, as I'm sure you don't want detention." Jason took her hand. "Don't worry about your parents, they will come around. It'll take some time, that's all. I'll work my charm on them. That'll help speed up the process. I'll show them that I'm worthy for you, that they can pass on the torch to me without fear of it going out."

"Jesus. You make me feel like I'm a possession."

"You are to them. You're their precious jewel."

All this heavy talk had given her indigestion. Maybe she shouldn't have had all that spicy food earlier. "Can we talk about this later?"

"Absolutely. How about I take you to a nice restaurant after work? The Bella Toni off Record Street? That'll be nice and empty after eight."

"Can't we just go to the pub instead?"

"We can do that too, if you like."

"Thanks. Will you walk me to work?"

"That's the plan, Ellis."

CHAPTER FOUR
TWO MORE TO THE PARTY

She had five minutes left before that damn clock hit the magic number. Ellis wasn't sure if she could last that long. This new floor supervisor had really been on one today. Like it was their fault that the lads in fabrics on the floor below didn't bring up the printed cloth until three. Like it was their fault that one of the embossing cradles decided that today was the day when it decided to start smoking.

Four minutes to go. After today's crappy day, she wouldn't be all that shocked if she decided to start smoking. Her mate on this line had done exactly that. She'd taken advantage of the floor supervisor's unfamiliarity with the staff to pull the woman's problem excuse on him. What a load of shite. She would be on the fire exit gantry right now, desperately sucking away on those sticks, getting as much out before the factory sirens sounded.

From the way he spun around and the shocked expression appearing on Dennis Howard 's face, Ellis figured that the young man had finally noticed he had a worker missing. It was either that or the management phone drums had just informed him the company's upper floor suits were on their way down. She didn't care either way. It's not like any of the others on this level would grass on Lorraine. As for the possible appearance of a suit, Ellis hoped to be out of here by then.

Right on cue, the siren blared, signalling the end of her last shift until Monday. She left her station and followed the others towards the exit at the far side of the factory, while being thankful that Dennis was on the other side, speaking into his work phone. The shocked look had yet to leave his face. Ellis guessed he was receiving a major bollocking for not getting the order out before the end of shift.

A lot of her fellow workers didn't have many flattering words to say about the poor sods on the next tier up who had the stressful task of keeping them under control. They moaned about them being paid twice as much as them or complained that none of the shop-floor staff were allowed to keep their purses, wallets or mobile phones on them while working. According to some of the more vocal, working here was worse than prison, that schoolkids were treated with more respect.

Ellis wouldn't want their job, and she was willing to bet twenty quid that her fellow gobby workers wouldn't last five minutes. Not without twatting one of the suits. She beat a hasty retreat when Dennis started calling people back, asking for weekend volunteers. Ellis might feel sorry for the likes of Dennis, but she sure as hell wasn't going to be guilt tripped into doing any overtime.

Lorraine leaned against her locker, looking like the cat who had got the cream. She shifted to the left to allow Ellis access to her locker. "Did he notice me missing?"

She shrugged. "I don't think so, Lorraine. Hard to tell with that one."

Her friend chuckled. "Don't bet on it, lady. He knows exactly what I look like."

She stared at Lorraine for a good five seconds, while deciding what she could mean by that rather cryptic reply. In the end, Ellis decided to drop it, not wishing to know what she meant by that.

Of all her vocal co-workers, Lorraine Chambers really did have the loudest voice, always finding daily faults in either their supervisors, the suits or the place itself, especially the supervisors. What surprised Ellis was that out of work, Lorraine had to be the kindest, warm-hearted individual that you could ever hope to meet.

Ellis opened her locker. There was definitely some kind of Jekyll and Hyde issue kicking off in that woman's mind. She removed her phone and bag and closed the locker door. "Got some news by the way," she confided, deciding it was best to tell Lorraine about Jason's idea rather than finding out that her best mate had been sleeping with Kevin, or whatever her cryptic phase was supposed to mean.

The thought of those two coupling was enough to make Ellis lose what remained of her spicy meal but it might not be that far from the truth. Lorraine Chambers lived with one teenage son on the other side of town. Lewis was either at his mates or with his dad, meaning she had the place to herself for most of the time. Lewis tended to go against the general flow of staying at home, plugged into consoles and PC's. He obviously inherited that trait from his mum, along with his good looks. Lorraine was no dog, that's for sure and although she was almost two decades older than Ellis, nobody would ever guess, not with how she acted.

Why was Ellis attracted to all these 'can do' type of people?

Had Lorraine really taken Kevin back to her place for a jolly old time between the sheets or was her imagination playing up again? More to the point, was it any of her business? Lorraine had been the one who had taken that seventeen year old girl under her wing and taught Ellis the ropes. Granted, most of the time, this meant showing her how to avoid working but still, in those days Lorraine was the only mate she had.

Those bright blue eyes opened a little wider. "Oh crap! Don't tell me that you and Jason are splitting up?"

"What? No, of course not. For Christ's sake, Lorraine, why do you have to assume everything's going to be a sodding disaster?"

"It's this place," she replied. "You know it brings out the worst in me. Come on then, spit it out. What are you so dying to tell me?" Lorraine walked over to the staff exit, moving to the left to allow a couple of workers to pass her. She zipped up her jacket. "Ellis. Come on, don't keep me in suspense."

Ellis passed her friend, took in a lungful of cold autumn air then waved at Marty, who was waiting for them outside the bus shelter. "Jason has his heart set on renting this market stall. I'm not keen, to be honest.

"As much as I hate this job, the shitty hours, the crap money, it's at least regular, you know? I mean the hours might be shitty, but there's enough of them to ensure I get a half-decent wage at the end of the month."

She gazed at Lorraine, trying to gauge how she'd react. Ever since the two had met, this woman had never stopped banging on about leaving here and getting something better. Back in the early days, Ellis believed the older woman would be leaving at any moment. When the weeks turned into months and the tune never changed, Ellis began to wonder if Lorraine's job searching was only in her mind. She wasn't so much of a 'can do' girl in that regard.

"In the market, you say?"

She nodded.

"He pointed the place out to you while it was full of folk shopping?"

"Yes, for crying out loud. Wait, what are you grinning at?"

"Well, I sure hope that you wrapped your arms around that manly chest and gave the hunk a nice big kiss before screaming out 'yes, I will, my lover'. You know, as loud as you can."

"Shut up, you're bloody mental."

"I know I would have."

"You serious?"

"About french kissing your boyfriend? Too right I am." She chuckled. "Joke." Lorraine closed the gap between her and Marty. "Guess what? Ellis is going to start selling e-cigs in the market." Lorraine winked at the third member of their group. "Best get your orders in now. She's doing a discount for mates."

"You can count me out. I can't be bothered with all that posing shite. I'll stick to the good old-fashioned cancer sticks, thank you very much. I don't see the point of them myself."

"Lorraine, will you give it up!" She placed her hands on her hips. "For one thing, it's Jason's idea, not mine and second," Ellis sighed, dropped her arms and looked at her feet. "And second, I still haven't made up my mind."

"This had better be a joke, girl!" said Lorraine. "One big wind up. I meant it, you know, when I said you ought to bite off your boyfriend's hand. Hell, I wish I had someone like him to look after me." She glanced over at Marty. "That's not an invitation, by the way."

Marty chuckled a couple of times. "Lorraine, sweetheart. We've been over this millions of times. I'm way out of your league." He hurriedly jumped back onto the path when a couple of cars pulled out of the car park and drove past the three of them. "Ellis, just fill in a couple of blanks for me here. What exactly did your fella say to you at lunchtime? About this market stall, I mean."

"Well, we met up, as per usual, then he takes me through the market and stops at the dilapidated old shack. I saw this huge grin on his face and it didn't take that much figuring out what he was planning. You know, that he wanted to rent it and..." Ellis paused. "I'm sorry, it just all felt kinda rushed. I mean, he's never said anything about wanting to run a stall before."

"I understand your concerns, Ellis. Really I do, and perhaps you should be talking about this more with your fella."

"Thanks, I was going to do that."

"Good girl."

Marty Price worked in accounts, she and Lorraine usually only saw him either at lunchtime or just after work. Ellis had known him for about as long as she'd known Lorraine. She still remembered her first day, when her new friend pulled her into the staff canteen and made a beeline towards a table where this diminutive, grey-haired thin man sat alone, quietly munching on a sandwich. Introductions were made and, to her surprise, this man who had to be twice her age, actually talked to her like an adult. He was genuinely nice to her too. They did make a strange trio, that's for sure. Ellis had even confided in Marty over the constant troubles she had with her pretend parents. It was odd looking back at his advice, she realised it wasn't that different to what Jason had said to her this lunchtime.

"There's no reason why you can't do both," said Marty. "Nobody says you can't keep this job and help him out at weekends. If the business venture does take off, then simply drop a few hours here. That way, you still have your security blanket. It's a win-win situation."

"I never thought of that. Thanks!"

"Don't mention it. What does he want to sell on it, by the way? If you're allowed to tell me, that is."

"Come on. You know Jason, what do you think?"

He pretended to chew over her words. "Erm, would it be toys by any chance?"

She nodded. "You've hit the nail on the head. Old toys, you know, stuff that you probably used to play with. No offence."

"None taken."

Marty reached a pedestrian crossing and pressed the button. As per usual, Lorraine just waited for a gap in the traffic then ran over.

"I bet this has been plaguing your thoughts ever since you got back."

Ellis shrugged. "I suppose so."

"You shouldn't let stuff like this worry you too much. Your bloke is a decent catch. He has never struck me as the kind of guy who goes around making decisions, if that's what you're concerned about." He reached the other side of the road. "Oh, and speak of the devil, look who Lorraine has found."

Jason had been waiting for her, perched on top of a six-foot brick wall, next to a furniture shop. Lorraine had taken the opportunity to grab his left leg while pretending to pull him off the wall. Anybody else watching would believe it was those two who were going out with each other. Watching the pair of them giggle and fight like kids kinda made her a little bit jealous. Ellis then felt guilty for allowing that emotion to get a foothold.

"Oh dear. I think we had better rescue your young man before Lorraine decides to stuff him into a pocket and make a break for it."

"Okay, you grab Lorraine and hold her in place so I can run off with Jason."

Marty laughed. "Can't I run off with Jason instead? He's more my type."

"I'll fight you for him," she replied, joining in with his laughter. "Wait, no. Forget that. If we started scrapping, Lorraine would just take advantage."

He nodded. "Yeah, and ruin him for you." Marty took her hand. "Come on, let's get those two separated. We'll try using sticks. If that fails, it'll have to be a bucket of water." They were halfway across the road when another tremor slammed into them. The road under Marty 's feet opened up. Ellis screamed when the older man fell into the new chasm, taking her with him. Her body slammed against the road surface but she still kept her fingers tight around his hand.

"Oh, God. Help us!"

The other two were already on their way. Jason dropped to the floor, reached down and grabbed Marty's other arm, while Lorraine helped Ellis by offering the stricken man her arm, which he took, once Jason had secured him.

"Okay, Lorraine. Help me get him up." Jason pulled him out of the chasm, put Marty's arm around his shoulder and carried him safely to the other side of the road.

Lorraine escorted Ellis across and sat her next to the shaking man. "Fuck me," she gasped. "That was pretty intense!" Lorraine crouched in front of the older man. "How are you holding up, Marty? I mean, if you want to puke, just lift your finger in the air or something as I sure as hell don't want any of your puke on my shoes. I remember what you had for your lunch."

He shook his head. "As considerate as always, dear."

"That's me all over."

Jason bent down and kissed the top of Ellis's head. "I won't be a moment."

"Where are you going?" she asked, looking up.

"I spotted a bunch of people earlier on. I just want to make sure that they are okay too."

Ellis stood up. "I'm coming too."

Marty grabbed Lorraine and used her to help himself up. "Best we all go then," he muttered. "As I'm sure as hell not staying here by myself while your hunky boyfriend finds some other helpless man to rescue."

"You do know he's taken, Marty?"

He smiled at Ellis. "An old man can dream you know."

The terror of what just happened hung around the back of her head like some cloaked demon, it looked like it was going to take up residence. From the drawn expression etched on Marty's face, she guessed that he felt pretty much the same. What they all needed right now was a few buckets of anything alcoholic. Yet, Ellis dare not voice this for fear that it might sound selfish. After all, Jason was right. They had a duty to make sure anyone else was okay too. She took Marty's hand and kissed his cheek. "When we finally get to the pub, Jason can buy the first round. His treat."

The man in question had slowed down then stopped in the middle of the road. Ellis let go of Marty and joined him. She followed his gaze and saw that this chasm continued all the way along the road, ending abruptly when grass replaced tarmac. There wasn't another soul to be seen or heard. As stupid as it sounded, it honestly felt like they were the only people left alive. "Where is everybody?"

Jason shrugged.

"They're all in the sodding pub," replied Lorraine. "Which is exactly where we should be right now." She tapped Jason on the shoulder. "Your pretty girlfriend is right, it is your turn to buy the first round."

CHAPTER FIVE
EXPLORERS FROM ANOTHER WORLD

The relentless screaming had been the worst part but, thankfully, the noise died down a few minutes ago. Denise Appleby then felt like an utter shit for putting her feelings above somebody else who had needed much more help than she did.

Her friend, Mandy Price, moved away from the body and sat back down in her allocated spot. Denise believed the tears were about to start once again. She found it a little hard to believe that such a frail woman could hold so much eye water. The woman should have used up her last reserves when the ceiling at the far end of the café came down on top of that young family. That was after the last tremor which brought down the shop's ornate frontage, effectively ensuring that escape through the main entrance was impossible.

Looking back, the remaining nine people in here should have left through the fire-door like the scruffy boy and some teen girl had the moment the tremor struck. That might have happened if the middle-aged man sat closest to the front door hadn't slumped forward, landing face first in Gloria's Café special of mushy peas, steak pie, gravy, and mash. Denise, along with Mandy and some of the other customers rushed over to see if he was alright.

He wasn't alright, far from it. The man had died. Mandy said he must have had a heart attack. At this news, the other customers took a single step back, as if they believed that death was contagious. It was left to her to pull him back and wipe as much of the food as she could from his face. At that point, Gloria rushed out from behind the counter and helped Denise with the clearing up. She politely asked the customers to leave the shop, via the fire-door, before gazing at Denise and asking her to do the same. She didn't move and neither did the others. It had to be the strangest situation she had ever been in. When it became clear that Denise wasn't going to leave her, Gloria started saying that she'd been onto the council for years about the state of the outside of her shop. Naturally, she blamed it on the car exhaust, convinced that all that foul black smoke ate the stone like acid.

Denise cleared away the last of the mashed potato from under his chin, refusing to scoop out the mushy peas that had gone up his nostrils. She left the table and walked over to her friend who had joined the others in watching her and Gloria during the macabre cleaning operation. The café owner continued to bad mouth the council. Denise wasn't sure if the other woman had even noticed that she had left the table. It had to be shock. The woman's way of coping with such a terrible situation. Denise coped by singing a children's song under her breath.

She grabbed her friend's hand. Gave the weeping woman a comforting smile and patted her hand before looking back at the protruding body parts sticking out from under the rubble. "There were six in the bed and the little one said..."

Denise was probably going to hell if they didn't get out of this. She heard scuffling, turned around and found that Gloria had made them all another cup of tea. At least they weren't going to run out of that any time soon, or food for that matter. The last of the air was probably going to be what took them. Still, considering they'd been stuck in here for at least half an hour, the air still seemed okay. How much air could a room this size hold anyway? Denise thanked the lady and took a single sip, grimacing once more at the amount of sugar the woman had given her. You always gave someone suffering from shock hot, sweet tea. Heck, Denise even recalled saying that piece of old rubbish to her daughter back when her good for nothing husband fell off the house roof. He broke his leg in three places. As far as she was concerned, it couldn't have happened to a more deserving individual. Shame it hadn't been his neck.

"Do you want another tissue, dear?" she asked. "I think that one is ready for its funeral." Denise dug into her purse, pulled out a paper tissue and stuffed it into Mandy 's hand. "I think that you had better drink your tea as well. There's nothing worse than cold tea."

"What is wrong with you, Denise?" she sniffed. "How can you stay so calm about this? For crying out loud, woman. Can't you see that we're going to die in here?"

Denise caught a glance of the three remaining café survivors all looking up from their own misery and directing their attention towards her friend's slightly hysterical but most annoying raised vocal concern. These were the ones who silently stood there and watched her clean off that gunk from that poor man's face. The natural rubberneckers. She wasn't going to allow them to use her and Mandy for entertainment!

Denise stood up, pushed her tea into the middle of the table then squeezed past her friend. She walked past the others, over to the collapsed ceiling and kneeled down, beside an exposed hand that belonged to the young man. Denise gave that one a quick appraisal when he walked in, with the unhappy blond wife and the little boy in tow.

From the snippets of conversation she picked up, the woman and the boy wanted to go a burger joint. The man wasn't having any of that, oh no. He wanted to take them to the café where his mum used to take him when he was the same age as Trevor, and that was final. She heard the man's tone hardening and the woman's voice changing from annoyance to submissive in the time it took the man to find a table. Admittedly, it did peeve her to see the young woman give in so easily, she reminded her so much of Mandy. Denise put it to the back of her mind though, after all, it wasn't her life, shame really as Denise could have done so much with that man and his rather firm backside.

Looking at the still hand, covered in plaster dust, she kinda wished he had listened to his wife now. She managed to pick up a small piece of rubble, the size of a football and shifted it around, a little shocked that it weighed so much. Denise picked up a few more smaller pieces and moved them before glancing over her shoulder. As expected, the three onlookers were doing what they did best. "Are you seriously going to allow this frail old woman to dig us out all by herself? Have you no shame?" She glanced over at Mandy and caught her eye. "Unless, that is, you all really do want to die in here?"

They fell over themselves to come to her aid. The two teenagers, she suspected a couple of years younger than the dead man, dropped down at either side.

"Sorry, Mrs. I was going to help, I swear."

The remaining onlooker, a woman with dark brown hair, wearing an over-coat that smelled like an old dog had pissed in both pockets, helped Denise up.

"You're right, dear. We can't have you breaking your back. Let's get you sat back down with your friend so you can finish your cup of tea." The woman helped Denise back to the table and sat her back down next to Mandy before going back to helping the boys.

Mandy put her cup down and stared, open-mouthed at her. "One of these days, I'm going to work out how you do that."

"One of these days? Wait on, a minute ago, you were convinced that there wouldn't be any more days after this one. Changed your mind already have you?"

"No, of course I haven't. Come on, be serious here, Denise. Look at them. Those three might move all the small pieces but some of those lumps of stone must weigh as much as a small car. No," she announced. "We're not going to get out of here alive."

"Oh, and now you can predict the future?" Denise shook her head. "That is just so much rubbish, and you know it. Nobody knows what path our future is set upon. Honestly, of all the people I know, I thought you would have realised this by now." She arched her back, it might not have been a good idea to pick up that heavy lump. She might have just put her back out.

Gloria leaned over her shoulder, picked up the now empty cups and returned them to the counter. "The rescuers will dig us out soon, you mark my words. Would you two ladies like another cup of tea?"

Denise smiled back and shook her head. "I think we're both fine at the moment, dear. Thank you anyway." She waited for the other woman to vanish back behind the counter before looking back at Mandy. "You remember what happened to your Albert. I don't remember you predicting that one."

"Now that's not fair, Denise," she hissed. "So below the belt. Ugh, then again, what else should I have expected from you?"

She gave the woman a generic grin, pleased that her cutting remark had brought out a bit of fire. Although she didn't agree with her friend's proclamation of oncoming inevitable death, Denise did understand that the next few hours would indeed get a little hairy and having Mandy shivering in a corner would not do her any good at all. Denise needed her friend to be on the ball and unfortunately, she knew from past experience that getting her mad was the only way to do it. Not just past experience but painful experience too.

Denise and Mandy had known each other since school. They weren't friends back then, more like bitter enemies. Denise was ashamed to admit that back in her early years, she did tend to be a bit of a wild-child and that included bullying the kids who she happened to take an instant dislike to.

Her favourite target was a girl whose family had moved up from London a few months earlier. Mandy Laker, a little big for her age, incredibly shy and as dumb as an ox. At least, she was in Denise's opinion. Taking money off the girl and threatening to flush her head down the toilet made her day complete. That all stopped when on one particular sunny day, the new girl actually retorted by calling her a 'nasty cow'. Of course, Denise was having none of that and decided to teach her a lesson by really pushing the girl's fat head down the toilet bowl. Only, the situation didn't quite go to plan, as Denise saw another side to Mandy once they were alone in the girl's toilets and the new girl knocked seven shades of shit out of her and, as an after-thought, pushed Denise's head down the toilet.

How they became friends, a few years after leaving school was a mystery to Denise but that's how it happened. Not just passing acquaintances either but best friends. Mandy even wanted Denise to go on their honeymoon but her then new husband, wasn't all that keen on the idea.

Albert Price attempted to drive a wedge between their friendship. Denise hadn't minded, not in the beginning anyway. All she wanted was for her friend to be happy and her new man did indeed make the woman very happy but not all fairytale weddings had a happy ever after ending. The cracks started to show just a month later when Mandy confided to Denise that Albert used to hit her. Denise, being the subtle person that she was, told the silly mare to hit him back. Heck, Mandy was three times the size of that scrawny man. One punch would knock him into next Wednesday. After that, the dirty weasel would soon see the error of his ways. Alas, it was not to be. Denise could only watch from the sidelines as her husband turned that happy and contented woman into the shell of the same person. He too, like the man sitting at the front of the café, suffered a heart attack but unlike the customer over there, Denise would have left that food on his face to rot.

It took Denise another decade to put right the damage that little fiend had caused to her best friend. "Okay, so that last remark about your husband was a bit uncalled for but I am right. Nobody had a clue that he was going to just keel over like that, especially not you."

"What has that got to do with anything, Denise?"

"I'm just saying, that's all. Nobody knows what's just around the corner. Heck, for all you know, a bunch of hunky rescuers could be, right now, on the other side of that rubble. Digging away, removing stones bit by bit, inching closer to us."

"Good grief, lady, do you never stop thinking about sex?"

Denise giggled. "You make it sound like that's a bad thing." She leaned across the table. "And don't you give me that face either, Mandy Price. I saw you staring at the young man in the market earlier on. You know, the one who was messing about on that children's ride."

"I don't know what you're talking about, all I was doing was telling him to stop acting like a child."

Her friend's red face told Denise a completely different story. "All you were doing was wondering how good he was in bed." She leaned back. "I know I was."

"You are unbelievable, Denise. At your age too. You ought to be ashamed of yourself."

"Well, guess what? I'm not. You shouldn't be either. Okay, so the man in the market was a bit too young, and I'm sure those hunky rescuers might be out of our league too but there are plenty of other desirable catches in our social circle. Men with a kind heart, who know how to look after us women of a certain age. You are rolling your eyes again, Mandy. I'm serious here." Denise looked over at the three other customers. Mandy was right about them, they really were getting nowhere. "You know what I'm going to do?"

Her friend shook her head. "I'm almost too scared to ask but I'm going to anyway. Go on, tell me what you are going to do."

Denise grinned. "When we get out of here, I am going to get us two hooked up. You know, just like we used to before you and Albert got wed."

"You cannot be serious. We're both sixty-eight, not twenty-two anymore! I probably wouldn't even know what to do with a man anymore." Mandy looked across at the three diggers. "There are times when I seriously wonder about you, Denise."

There were times when she seriously wondered about herself too. She watched the two teen boys attempt to pull on a stone twice the size of her head; it wasn't budging, despite their efforts. Denise then noticed that one of the boys had covered up that hand with a red plastic table cloth. She refused to believe that their time had come, that within the next few hours when the air started to run out, that she'd be on the floor, wheezing and slowly suffocating and thinking that the young family really had been the lucky ones after all. Well, the man anyway. It took his wife a long time to die.

The irony of it all was, just like that young family, if she had not been such a stubborn old bag, and listened to her friend and grabbed a cup of tea at one of those cheaper ethnic places in the market instead of dragging Mandy up to this old café, then they wouldn't be in this dreadful situation either.

Mandy suddenly jumped up, her chair tipped backwards. The woman tapped the table twice then clasped her hands together. "Can you hear that, Denise?" She hurried over to the collapsed section, realised that her friend wasn't with her and ran back, physically pulled Denise out of the chair and pulled her over. "What about now?"

The three other customers had all stopped what they were doing and the only sound that Denise could now hear did indeed come from the other side of that rubble and it did sound like a bunch of hunky workmen attempting to dig them out!

"Oh, Lord, Denise, I'm so sorry for doubting you!" Her friend took Denise back to the chair and sat her down. "You just rest here, honey. We'll be out in a jiffy, I know we will. Oh, this is so exciting!"

She could not share her friend's enthusiasm. There was something so strange about the noises coming from the other side. For a start, Denise couldn't hear a single voice. No shouting, no asking if anyone was in there, not even the generic guy stood at the back, shouting that everything was going to be alright. Whoever it was were not using anything mechanical either. The sound was all wrong for that. If anything, it sounded more like claws scrabbling against rock. Could the rescuers be using dogs? Denise heard something else too. It was faint but it was there. It sounded like clicking.

The sound of a sudden rockfall reached her ears. The other three on the edge of the collapsed wall all gasped as one but then cheered. Denise saw why, a tiny hole had appeared just above the woman's head, letting in a bright spear of natural light. Denise thought that it had to be one of the most beautiful things she had ever seen.

Gloria rushed past their table, holding a tray laden with biscuits, pastries and chocolate. She placed that on the nearest table then joined the other three in helping to shift some more of the rubble. By now, two more small holes had appeared.

The scrabbling noise became more urgent. It certainly didn't sound like hunky rescuers valiantly trying to save them now. Even the four right at the front had moved back a couple of paces. Mandy grabbed Denise's hand. That clicking noise overwhelmed just about every other noise! That is, until their rescuers made an appearance.

The return of the relentless screaming blasted from the two boys as something thick, long and brown pushed through one of the ever widening holes. It unfurled to reveal several pale cream serrated hooks. The closest boy attempted to jump away as the arm moved towards him, but as soon as he moved, the top part, containing those hooks flipped out on a flexible hinge. Three of the hooks sunk into the boy's torso and pulled the shrieking individual closer to the hole.

The other boys ran forward, grabbed the screaming boy's left arm and tried to pull him back to safety. He too ended up in the same predicament when the holes joined up and two more of those long pole-like objects pushed through, each one unfurled, revealing their deadly cargo. The hooks from both poles slammed into the sides of the second boy's head. His movements immediately stilled. The screaming intensified as both Gloria and Mandy joined in with the chorus when the owners of those long brown poles finally made an appearance.

It looked like some kind of praying mantis, but this one was the size of a car! It wasn't alone either, as two more giant creatures were attempting to burrow through the remaining rubble, obviously eager to dine on the trapped humans. They looked just like beetles but as with the other monster, these things were enormous.

Denise briefly wondered if she had gone insane or if Gloria had put something weird in her tea. She also couldn't understand why she felt so fucking calm about the situation. The woman in question, the owner of the café, attempted to rescue the remaining woman when one of the beetles snagged her foot, only for the other beetle to reach through one of the wider holes. Its jaws closed around the woman's ankle and neatly snipped off her foot.

Her friend had sensibly run back to where Denise sat. The look on the poor woman's face told her that Mandy obviously wanted her to do something. Like there really was anything they could do, except to await their demise. The praying mantis had finished with the boys, eating everything, including their bones. All that remained were a few shreds of clothing and a single trainer.

Denise leaned forward, expecting it to pull the now dead Gloria through the gap but, no. It turned on its two companions. It obviously felt that having a pair of ravenous, armour-plated insectile killing machines eating what it probably thought was its food felt too much like competition. Although the beetles easily made short work of the remaining woman, neither giant insect stood a chance against the mantis. Those hooked claw cracked their shells in several places to reveal their soft, gooey, vulnerable insides to the other monster's jaws.

It then turned its attention to Mandy and Denise. The mantis pushed its head through the widest hole and continued to push. Even from where she sat, Denise saw cracks appearing around the edges of the hole.

"What are we going to do now? cried her best friend.

"There were two in the bed, and the little one said..."

CHAPTER SIX
MAKING A WITHDRAWAL

He was aware that the world had turned upside down. He heard shouting, a panicked cry, as well as the sound of a sharp slap. The landscape beyond the confines of their now fucked up car had, thankfully, righted itself by the time that Andrew Davis had re-joined the land of the living.

That last tremor really had knocked him for six.

"I think we might have to make a few alterations to our plans, boss. Have you seen this?"

Andrew opened his eyes, brushed broken glass off his lap, then gingerly stretched his arms and rotated his neck. It didn't feel like anything was broken, apart from the car, that is. He turned his neck and peered out of the smashed back window, trying to work out what had caused the car to spin like that. It was only when he leaned to the side that the reason became clear. "Bloody hell!" he gasped. "That is just unreal."

"Tell me about it," replied Nelson. "It took me by surprise as well. I had to fight this twatting steering wheel for control of the car. To be honest, we were lucky to escape unharmed." He glared at his passenger. "Do you not have anything to say, Tony?" Nelson raised his hand, making the younger man flinch.

"Sorry, Guv."

"For?"

"For panicking and trying to grab the wheel off Nelson."

"Are we done?" Andrew turned his attention back to the gaping chasm running down the middle of the main street. It would take more than a few bollards and wooden-tops to sort out this mess. The emergency services would be up to their necks in work due to this, that's for sure, as Andrew doubted that they were the only accident to happen thanks to this. Andrew popped the seat belt, grabbed his bag of tricks and attempted to open the side door. The damn thing was stuck but a couple of vicious kicks soon sorted that. He climbed out of the car, stretched again then took a more detailed inspection of the damage.

The shops on the other side didn't look too badly damaged, apart from a few broken windows and some missing roof tiles. He turned around and spotted the same on the shops in front of him. There were a couple of hairline fractures around the windows and doors which might pose a problem. He stopped. Christ on a bike, he was turning into his old man here. David Davis, the best builder in Bradfield. At least, that's what Andrew's mum used to say.

He shook away the random memory and put his thoughts back where they belonged. The last thing he needed right now was to start going off at a tangent. Andrew leaned on the side of the car and watched an old woman burst out of a greengrocers on the other side of the road. She raced up the street then ran into a newsagents on the corner. The old bag had been going at a fair rate too, almost as if somebody was chasing her.

"Come on, you two. Out you get. We still have a job to do." He kicked the side door. His voice sounded so loud. That unnerved him a little. It wasn't silent in the street, but pretty close. A couple of car alarms were going off somewhere and he could hear somebody crying out for help but apart from that, there wasn't any other noise. Andrew paused. No, there was something else, something real faint. It sounded like somebody clicking their fingers.

Nelson emerged from his side then helped Tony out. The old man reached back inside, pulled out Tony's leather satchel and threw it at him. "What did I tell you earlier about keeping this with you?"

"Sorry."

"Yeah, sure you are."

Tony leaned back inside the car and pulled out a black balaclava. He placed it on his head and started to rolled it over his face when Nelson stopped him. "What the fuck are you playing at?" he demanded.

"What? I don't want any fucking clown to see my bastard face!"

"Come on, man. Use what little brain you have." Nelson nodded at Andrew then tapped the side of his head. "Do you see us two donning our masks?" He held up his hand. "No don't answer that, I'll tell you. It's cos it might look a little bit suspicious to any passer-by to observe three masked individuals walking down the street heading to the bank."

"Don't talk to me like a retard, I know that."

"And yet, there you were, putting on the mask. Look, man, don't worry, there are no cameras around here and I think the locals have more important things to worry about."

"Cut it out, guys," said Andrew. "Can you hear that weird noise?" Both men shook their heads. It had stopped anyway. Andrew wondered if he had imagined it. "Exactly. No sirens."

Nelson nodded. "Oh yeah! After what happened here, this place ought to be crawling with bizzies and firemen as well as paramedics. Makes me wonder what else has happened to warrant their absence?"

"It doesn't matter, does it? Just means the risk factor has just decreased to almost nothing." Andrew chuckled to himself. "I like those odds." The Black Lotus branch they were going to hit was another two streets away. He didn't mind the short walk but after the job, they'd need another set of wheels; even with a low police presence, sauntering down the high street with bags of cash slung over their shoulder would be the height of folly. "We need a car, Tony. As quick as you like, go for something old but decent, you know what I mean?"

The young man nodded, "Consider it done, boss. I know just where to go as well." He tapped his satchel while glaring at Nelson. "Oh yeah, I know exactly where to go." He spun around and ran back the way they had come.

That clicking noise was back again. Andrew turned and ran across the road. He leaped over the chasm and stopped in front of that greengrocers. It was coming from inside that shop. None of the lights were on and the sunlight could not penetrate the gloom. He felt like over a dozen set of eyes were watching him and for the first time in years, every hair down his spine stood upright. There was something not altogether right, lurking in the darkness, something that meant him and anybody else great harm. Something not human. Andrew was almost ready to reach for his pistol and to enter the shop when the clicking abruptly vanished again. The feeling of being watched disappeared at the same time.

"Hey, what are you doing?"

Andrew sighed heavily. He wasn't sure how to answer that as he didn't really know. Maybe he'd started to hear things that weren't there, on top of having random thoughts? He turned away from the shop and walked over to where Nelson stood. Maybe the stress of what they were about to pull off was having an adverse effect on him?

The old man stood by the edge of the chasm, leaning over and gazing down. Nelson didn't appear to be suffering from any after effects from either the crash or the tremor and he certainly didn't look in any way worried about robbing a bank. Then again, why should he? This wasn't Nelson's first hold up.

"Why did you run off?"

"Nothing, it was nothing. I thought I saw someone I knew. Turns out it was just a shadow. Guess I'm a little jumpy."

Nelson looked up. "It sure is a long way down. It feels like it goes all the way to hell. I don't think I'd like to fall in."

Andrew chuckled. "Oh, you think?"

Nelson jumped across. "Hell no. It's probably where my ex-wife is, no doubt chewing off Satan's ear, the horrible bitch." He patted Andrew on the back. "Nothing wrong with being jumpy, mate. Nothing wrong with being cautious either. Even in these weird circumstances, you need to keep your wits about you. More so now, I guess. Disasters tend to make people act funny, more unpredictable. People need a routine."

"Why did Tony give you that look?"

"The slap, I reckon." Nelson looked back towards where their car lay. "I shouldn't have hit the boy but it was instinctive. If I hadn't got his hands off the wheel, we might have all ended up having tea with my ex-wife. Even so, I still shouldn't have hit him. I guess I'm not immune to all this unpredictable behaviour either." He shrugged. "Still, he'll get over it."

"Oh yeah? That's not what you said back at the house."

"Back then, I'd have said anything to stop you from cleaning me out."

Andrew grinned back, not believing a word the old man said. "The significant amount of money that we get from this job ought to cheer him up." He still remembered the kid giving him the same look when he bent his finger back. Apparently it was the same look which put the kid behind bars in the first place.

The story went that Tony and his current girlfriend had just left a takeaway when a group of teenagers blocked their path. One of the group, the largest one, demanded that Tony should hand the kebab to his brother while he took possession of Tony's pretty blond girlfriend. When the kid didn't move, apparently this gorilla then made the fatal mistake of reaching for the girl's purse. Tony responded by pulling a knife out of his back pocket and slamming the business end into the kid's guts.

The only reason why Tony didn't end up with attempted murder was solely because the knife missed all his vital organs and the girlfriend swore blind that Tony had wrestled the knife out of the gorilla's hands and the stabbing had been an accident. If he had been in the same situation, it's likely that Andrew would have killed them all.

The pair reached the designated street at the same time as Andrew picked out another noise. This one he did recognise. There was a car heading towards them. "Is that Tony?"

Nelson nodded. "From the way that the idiot is driving? Yeah, I reckon so."

A small blue hatchback sped along the road, its tyres dangerously close to the edge of that chasm. Andrew swore blind that the damn thing sped up the moment the driver caught sight of them. Nelson even took a couple of steps closer to the corner of the old stone building as the small car raced towards them but at the last moment, the driver applied the brakes and screeched to a halt beside the kerb.

"Could you have made any more fucking noise?" Andrew hissed, when Tony climbed out of the driver's side.

"Do we put our masks on now?"

"Shut it, Tony." Nelson patted down his own bag of tricks then turned to Andrew. "Okay. I'm ready. Let's do this..."

Andrew pulled him away from the kerb just as two suited men ran screaming from the bank. They ran straight across the road, just managing to leap across the chasm at the last minute due to the pair continuously looking over their shoulders. Just like the woman before, these jokers were acting like something was chasing them.

"What the fuck are they running from?"

Andrew couldn't answer Tony's question, nor did he bother. As far as he was concerned, it meant two fewer people to worry about. He ran over the road and stopped by the bank's entrance. Unlike the street, the interior was equipped with cameras yet none of them had been positioned to capture the entrance or the exterior. That seems a little odd but it's not like he intended to complain. Andrew took out his own balaclava. "Are you set?" The others too masked up and pulled out their weapons while Andrew unzipped his canvas holdall and pulled out an ancient sawn-off shotgun. Behind his mask, he saw Nelson's eyes widen. He hadn't told anybody about this baby.

In fact, both Andrew and Tony were the first people, aside from him, to see this for over ten years. He had actually found this back when he'd been all sweet and innocent, with its shells, buried at the back of a barn which once belonged to the Henderson family. Maybe not that sweet and innocent. Andrew certainly had enough sense to know that the gun wasn't legal and that bad men must have hidden it in the barn to pick up at a later date.

Andrew ran into the bank, grinning from ear to ear. The moment he held this gun, Andrew craved to be one of those bad men and now, here he was. "Nobody move a fucking muscle!" he yelled.

His grin fell off his face and his voice faltered when he found out the only people in the large foyer were his crew. He ran over to the glass counters and peered over. As far as he could see, there was nobody hiding under the wood panelling. Andrew's heart started beating even faster when he saw the door leading into the room behind the counter stood ajar. "Shit," he muttered. Those two men weren't customers. They must work here!

Nelson joined him. "I don't like this. I mean, I know there's been tremors and there's a huge crack in the ground but that shouldn't make people run like their lives depended on it."

"Or something was chasing them," added Andrew.

Tony grabbed the edge of the door. "What do we do now?"

Andrew pulled the door wider then pulled open a metal litter bin to make sure it wouldn't swing shut. He didn't think it would but he wasn't going to take any chances. "What do you think we're going to do, you idiot? Nothing has changed, apart from this situation has made our operation so much easier. Nelson, find the safe and do your stuff." He turned to Tony. "You need to bring the car right up to the entrance and stay there. Keep the motor running and stay frosty. No nodding off! This won't take any time at all."

The two men went about their allocated tasks, leaving him to collect the banknotes from the tills. If Tony was unable to get into the safe then whatever he found needed splitting three ways. He hoped that there'd be enough to warrant such a risky venture. Although Tony had boasted that he could open any bank safe, Andrew still had his doubts. He had heard whispers whilst inside that the man wasn't all that he was cracked up to be, that the only reason why Tony hadn't been sprung was because he'd fucked up a job in London. A job which a certain family was depending on in order to pay some outstanding debts.

It really was a wonder that Tony had lived at all and it was that alone which had given him the confidence to approach the old bastard in the first place. After all, if he really was as crap as the rumours suggested then the family would have simply put a bullet in his head.

He made a beeline for the first till draw, noting that it was already open. This discrepancy should have triggered even more internal alarm bells but it all went out of the window when he saw how much was in there. The damn thing was stuffed with notes. The next two till drawers were in the same condition. Andrew's alarm bells only sounded again when he spotted the blood. It wasn't just the occasional spatter. The stuff was everywhere. It honestly looked like someone had opened a vein and aimed it at the walls.

"What happened in here?" he asked. There were two more till drawers to check but to do that, Andrew needed to splash through all that mess. Natural greed got the better of him though. The quicker he got this done, the faster they'd all get out of this fucking abattoir. The stink had started to get to him too. Andrew held his breath, then splashed his way across the drenched carpet, feeling his bile rising when he noticed that it wasn't just blood down there. He saw indescribable lumps of fuck knows what floating through that thick mess.

The two remaining till drawers were almost empty which proved to him what happened when your eyes got bigger than your belly. He retreated, doing his best to wipe off as much mess as he could.

Andrew knew full well the amount of danger he was putting himself in. Whatever had made this mess obviously wasn't part of the usual wildlife to be seen around town, that's for fucking sure, yet he couldn't figure out why he wasn't running in the opposite direction, following those two bank tellers. He pushed this enigma to the back of his mind, zipped up the holdall, slung it over his shoulder and ventured further into the building in search of Nelson.

It didn't take him long to find the old man, as he was in the immediate corridor, flattened against the wall. Nelson was not alone either. Another suited man crouched at Nelson's feet. The mid-twenty blond individual didn't even look up when he stopped in front of the two. Andrew guessed he was too busy staring at the buff carpet and shaking to notice that the man holding a gun had been joined by another gun-wielding masked man. It then dawned on him that Nelson no longer wore his balaclava. What the hell was he playing at?

Before Andrew could get a single word out, his companion gestured not to make a noise. He snapped his arm forward, curled his fingers around Andrew's left tit and pushed him against the same wall, then pointed towards the open doorway, directly opposite Nelson and his new friend.

His annoyance at discovering that one of the crew had shown his face melted away when he saw what was inside that other room. He lifted the shotgun, only for Nelson to frantically shake his head.

"There's more than one in there," he hissed.

Andrew had absolutely no idea what was inside that other room, only that whatever it was, the damn thing was big. A dog maybe, or even a pig? He slapped Nelson's hand off him and inched closer towards the older man, trying to make as little noise as possible. Andrew trusted Nelson's advice. He was also aware that of all the years he had known the man, he had never shown the slightest hint of fear. Until now, that is. Nelson was clearly scared of whatever lay in that other room. He might not be shaking as much as Jelly Boy down there but it was definitely there.

"More than one what, Nelson?" he replied.

Jelly Boy began to sob before his companion had chance to respond. "Oh, God. They are nightmares. Fucking nightmares!" He stared straight at Andrew. "You've got to help me. Get me out of here!"

Jelly Boy's voice had risen in volume with each word spoken. By the time he reached the end of the sentence, the damn fool was fair shouting and no amount of kicking from Nelson could shut him up.

In the end, Nelson didn't have to describe Jelly Boy's nightmares as one of them pushed its way through the opening. Andrew's mind had some trouble with actually believing his eyes. "You have got to be fucking shitting me," he muttered. This had to be somebody's idea of a joke. Since when did beetles ever grow to the size of a small pony? That notion soon vanished when he spotted its curved fangs, both already thick with blood.

Andrew knew he had found the architect of the carnage he had seen in that other room. Nelson threw himself in front of Jelly Boy and fired off two shots. The reports in the confined space almost blew out his ears but it did nothing to the huge beetle. Its shell must be too thick for the bullets to penetrate.

"Do something!" screamed the man.

Andrew dropped to his knees, slammed the stock into his shoulder, aimed the weapon at the monster's underside and fired. The blast literally tore off the back of the creature, covering the walls, ceiling and the two other men with sloppy black gore and bits of carapace.

"Don't look so fucking happy with yourself, man." Nelson wiped several lumps of gore off his face, reached over the insect corpse and pulled Andrew to his feet. "There's another two in that room!"

Jelly Boy scarpered and Nelson chased after him. "Where the fuck are you going?" Andrew ran after the pair of them, acutely aware that they were moving further away from their car. He also knew that the old man wasn't wrong about the dead thing not being alone. Andrew glanced behind him. Two more giant beetle creatures were fighting amongst themselves. Andrew guessed that the winner got to eat their dead friend.

He swung the gun around just in case those huge things decided they preferred human meat over the flesh of their own kind.

Nelson paused beside another open door then returned to Andrew's position. "Come on. Stop fucking dawdling. We have to shift our arses!"

He was about to bollock the idiot for running in the wrong direction but Nelson had already left him. "Just typical." Andrew turned around and saw the victor was indeed tucking into the dead beetle. The thing had managed to flip the corpse onto its back. It buried its head deep into the ruined underbelly while four of its six legs attempted to stop the corpse from rocking as it fed.

That monster was not concerned with feasting on its dead buddy to give a shit about Andrew but that sure as fuck didn't apply to the loser. It hadn't fared well in the battle, losing two legs along with a fracture running down one side of its smooth brown shell but, even injured, the thing craved food! It wasn't that much of an idiot to tackle the other beetle. Then again, why should it when other tastier morsels were within distance? It squeezed past the thing that had hurt it, scuttling a little faster when the victor's head lifted from under the syrupy yellow mess but once the loser had crossed the threshold, the victor once more plunged its head back into the corpse.

Andrew backed away, keeping the shotgun trained at the thing's head. He only had one cartridge left in the chamber and knew that if that shot did little damage then he might as well kiss his arse goodbye. Not that he thought he'd have time to kiss it, those things were fast!

"I think I've found us a way out."

Thank Christ for that, Nelson had come back. The old man stood beside him. He trained his pistol at the advancing beetle while he held the bank clerk's neck with the other. Fresh blood streamed down the side of his face, bubbling out from a long cut above the man's eye.

Nelson noticed his gaze. "He shouldn't have run away."

Andrew shrugged. The old man had a point. "You found an escape route?"

"Yeah, Damien here was kind enough to point out an employee's entrance which leads into the market."

"Good man. So why the fuck are we still here?"

Nelson looked at Andrew, winked, then cracked Damien on the side of the head with the pistol and pushed him forward with his foot. The beetle literally dived on the dazed banker and thrust its thick fangs into the man's back.

"Are you fucking insane?"

"He saw my face," replied Nelson. "Are you going to stand there all offended or are you coming with me?"

He took one look at the beetle's mandibles stripping the wet flesh from the man's neck before hurrying towards Nelson's retreating form.

CHAPTER SEVEN
ANOTHER SECRET UNCOVERED

The moment she looked over Jason's shoulder and saw they had the place to themselves, Ellis just knew that the shit really had hit the fan. What the hell were they doing in here in the first place? Marty needed checking out. It was obvious, even with her limited compulsory one day work's first-aid course, that the poor guy was in shock. She wasn't the only one to pick this up. Lorraine had commented too but her so-called medical advice centred upon getting a stiff drink down his gob.

The others gravitated towards the bar leaving her next to the inner door, feeling a little confused, scared and alone. Watching Jason acting up in front of her workmates was not helping matters at all. Was she the only person in here who believed they stood on the edge of some unknown fucking disaster? Ellis collapsed into the nearest chair, took out her phone and placed it onto the table next to someone's half-drunk beer. She looked at the other tables and saw more glasses, most of them containing some kind of beverage. Ellis also noticed an untidy pile of coins on a table to the immediate left of the ladies, and even somebody else's phone on another table. That alone made the shakes return.

Lorraine grabbed the back of the chair opposite Ellis with one hand. "Girl, you really do look like shit. Here, this should help put you right." She placed a glass down on the table with the other hand then scraped the chair back and sat down. "Come on, don't just start at it, get the stuff down your neck."

It shocked Ellis to discover that she wasn't alone in thinking they were all teetering on the edge of disaster. Under that thin layer of compassion, she saw the same ragged and extreme emotions carved on Lorraine's face too. It smelled like scotch. Ellis hated the stuff but still dragged the glass closer. "I look like shit? Have you looked in a mirror recently?" She picked up the glass and downed the lot in one go. The contents burned down her throat but she hardly noticed.

Lorraine tapped the table next to the phone. "I tried mine while your fella helped himself to the drinks. There's nobody about you see. Marty tried too. There's no service. Marty thinks the last tremor must have knocked out the two transmission towers. Seriously, I ask you. Who in their right mind builds a town inside a deep valley?"

She folded her own hand over Lorraine's while pressing the menu button on the phone which Jason bought her for Christmas. Oh hell, she had no service either. Her phone had suddenly turned into a brick. "I think I need another drink, Lorraine."

"You know, I expected this place to be full. Sure, I guess the place would have emptied when that quake hit, but I thought they would have returned, at least to pick up their dropped stuff. There's a wallet on the floor over there, Ellis."

"You don't think they all went home, do you?"

Her friend shrugged.

"You think they're dead?" In her mind, Ellis pictured over a dozen drunk customers piling out of the pub doors and falling straight into that crack in the ground, like lemmings falling off a cliff edge. "No, forget what I just said, that's stupid. More than likely they'll be staggering home. They'll have probably already forgotten why they left the pub in the first place." Ellis forced out a quiet laugh which sounded so fake, even to her ears. "You know what this place is like, Lorraine. The locals would have been lined up outside the door the moment they opened up."

"We haven't passed a single soul since this tremor hit us though." Lorraine stood up. "Not a single soul." She gently pulled Ellis out of the chair. "Come on, we had better get to the bar before Marty drinks the place dry. Don't forget your phone."

Jason had found the black leather wallet and had placed it on the bar along with several other items, including some coins, another three phones and a key fob. He looked up from his collection when Ellis approached and gave her a smile. "How are you holding up?"

"I've had better days. What are you doing?"

"I'm trying to figure out what happened in here," he replied. Jason pulled a bank card from the wallet, read the name then put it back. "With little success. Nothing adds up."

"What do you mean?"

"Come on, Ellis. We've been in here a few times after you've finished work. You know what this place is like. You know, loud, busy, and generally busy." Jason walked over to Ellis and gently placed his hands on the woman's shoulders and turned her around. "Just look at the pub. Does it seem a little too neat?"

"Oh heck!" Marty put his drink down. "Why didn't I see this? Ellis. Picture this pub, happy pissed voices shouting for attention at the bar. Couples sat at tables, mixing with the under-aged teens and the groups of buddies, all generally having a great time." He took a quick sip of his drink. "And then that tremor reverberates through the town. There would be panic, screaming, people running about, all trying to get the hell out of here before the building collapses on them."

It finally clicked. "Oh, I get you now. Where's the tipped chairs and broken glasses?"

Jason turned her back around. "Not to mention the lack of blood and closed fire-doors. I seriously doubted they all trooped out of the main door as calm as you like."

Lorraine checked her phone once more. "Jason, I don't think I'm all that turned on by your serious outlook. Look it's a bit weird, okay, I get it, but we're not the sodding Scooby gang." She re-filled her glass and drunk it in one go. "I think I'm going to head home now. A hot bath, a bottle of wine and TV is calling to me." Lorraine walked towards the door. "Catch you on the other side, kids. Marty, look after yourself."

"What the hell was that about?" Ellis attempted to run after her friend, only for Jason to stop her.

"Marty, would you mind doing the honours?"

The older man gave Jason a salute, grabbed the bottle of spirits and ran after Lorraine. "I'll see you outside."

"I should have kept my big mouth shut," he muttered. Jason threaded his way through the tables, heading to the far side of the pub. He stopped, bent down and picked something off the floor before making his way back to Ellis. "She's scared. I mean, really scared."

"And I'm not?"

"I know you are, honey, but you have always come across as a fairly stable person. Lorraine, despite the happy-go-lucky façade is nothing of the kind." He examined what he'd found on the floor. "If I'm right about this, then that poor girl is about to find herself being pushed to the very edge of insanity."

"If you are trying to scare me then it's bloody working!" The man she originally fell in love with had vanished. Everything, from his easy smile to his calm demeanour had changed. "Wait, what did you find over there? Another wallet?"

He shook his head. "No, not exactly." Jason opened his fingers. "This tells me that we should get away from here as soon as possible. In fact, I think we ought to get to my place as quickly as we can."

She looked at the object nestled in his palm and had no idea at all what it could be. It did look a little like a stick of raw asparagus but brown and segmented in the middle. An unpleasant smell drifted from it, reminding her a little of over-boiled cabbage mixed with wet dirt. "Do I even want to know what that is?"

He shook his head, dropped it on the floor, then reached into his inside jacket pocket. Before he pulled his hand out, Jason leaned forward and kissed Ellis on the lips. "I'm really sorry about this, honey. You really need to believe me on that."

"I don't understand."

"There are some aspects of me that I hoped you'd never have to experience." Jason slowly pulled out his hand which now contained a large black, automatic pistol. He took her hand then pulled Ellis over to the entrance, while looking over his shoulder. "Time to go."

A dozen questions all fought to be heard but she couldn't get even one out. A blistering scream coming from outside the pub shattered the relative silence. Both doors flew open and Marty ran inside, with Lorraine right behind her.

"You don't want to know what we just saw crawling out of the chasm!" he said, breathlessly.

"Do you think it saw us?"

Marty shook his head. "I don't think so."

"What is it?" Ellis pulled her hand from Jason's grip and ran over to the window. She climbed onto the red leather seat, pressed her nose against the glass and immediately wished she'd stayed in the dark. Her worst nightmare personified were crawling out of the wide crack and moving, very slowly, across the empty roads.

Bugs, dozens of them, all types and all super-sized. The smallest, a bright yellow locust thing was about the size of a greyhound but that particular specimen was a dwarf compared to some of them out there. "What the fuck is going on?" She looked back at her gun toting boyfriend. "Did you know about this, Jason?"

"Come on, Ellis!" cried Marty. "What sort of a question is that?"

"Did you not notice the evil looking bang bang in his hand?"

"We really need to get away from here," said Jason. "You have no idea how much danger we're in right now."

Ellis turned back to the window. "Forget it. There's no chance that I'm going outside with those things running about. Anyway, none of them appear to be coming towards us." The exodus from the chasm had slowed down. A couple more locust things crawled onto the road surface and skittered away, followed by a black beetle. That was about the same size as the locust thing but looked way more dangerous. Jason did have a point though, they couldn't stay in here for any length of time. Maybe they could escape those bugs? Despite their size, it didn't look like they were able to move with any speed.

Her hopes of escape were soon dashed when Ellis saw that the streets weren't as empty as she first believed. An old man pulled his body out from under a dark-blue delivery truck and slowly crawled on his hands and knees towards one of the town-centre's remaining telephone boxes. It took her a moment to figure out who it was.

David Hayes, a regular to the top market, not that any of the usual customers would normally see him. He was generally spotted going through the trade bins in the large compound behind the market. The only reason she knew of his nocturnal habit was because of listening to Aroon complaining about the mess he made, and the fact that his father always got him to tidy it up. Aroon once told Ellis that he believed that the tramp must have been a spider in some past life as it was the only thing that could explain how such a scrawny looking old man was able to scale a seven-foot stone wall, topped with razor wire.

Ellis soon understood how Hayes was able to scramble over that market wall when a green and yellow striped bug scurried close to the man. He raced over to the side of a double-decker bus on the other side of the road and, using the door mechanism, the side mirror and an open window on the top deck, was able to reach the roof before the giant insect had realised its food had just escaped.

Not that this helped David. As soon as he had gone from crawling to running, every insect in sight reacted and Ellis saw, to her horror, that the bastard things weren't quite as slow as she first believed. They rushed en-mass towards the stationary vehicle at an astonishing speed, surrounding the bus in seconds.

"Oh my God!"

Ellis hadn't noticed both Marty and Lorraine had joined her to watch this macabre show.

"We have to do something to help that poor man," continued Marty. "It won't take them long to get to him."

She believed that Marty could be right. A couple of the smaller ones had taken advantage of the predators squashed against the bus sides by jumping on their backs. David had to run down the length of the roof to escape their claws.

"What can we do?"

"I'm sorry, there's nothing we can do. It's best that you don't see this. Ellis, please, can you come away from the window?"

It looked like David could be safe after all as the large monsters hadn't taken too kindly to being used as ladders. They pulled the smaller animals down then savagely ripped them apart. Pieces of broken shell, torn legs and yellow and red fluid went flying. The new movement shifted the attention from David as the giant insects all converged on the shifting, wet mass of hard bodies, no doubt all eager to get a piece of their now deceased comrades.

Jason pushed in between Lorraine and Ellis. "Please, we so need to get away from here. I can't stress enough that moving from this location will be our wisest choice."

"Are you having a laugh?" Lorraine pointed to the bus. "You saw how fast those things can move. We won't last five minutes out there."

"Oh God! Please tell me that I'm imagining that!"

Ellis followed Lorraine's gaze and saw three of those giant locusts had flown up to the top of the Black Lotus bank. They perched on the roof edge and it was obvious they were about to fly next. Sure enough, they spread their wings and took off, heading straight for the roof of the bus. Ellis finally took Jason's advice and looked away but that didn't stop her from hearing the poor man's frantic cries for help, soon followed by his very noisy death.

She allowed Jason to take her in his arms. "What are we going to do?"

"We do what we should have done in the first place." He gently unpeeled her from his torso. "This is all my fault. I should have known they were going to emerge. It's..." he shook his head. "Never mind. Come on. Follow me." He pulled her back through the pub. Lorraine and Marty followed.

For the first time in months, Lorraine actually kept her mouth shut. Ellis kinda wished her friend kept talking; watching Lorraine's face going through a kaleidoscope of expressions, all of them bad, fucking terrified her.

Jason took them through the bar area and into the reception. He stopped next to a code-locked door, pushed in a six digit combination, then pushed the handle down. The door opened. Ellis didn't bother asking how he could possibly know some random door code. Too much had happened already today and the whole situation stopped making much sense hours ago. Hell, once the giant insects made their dramatic entrance, everything went into free-fall.

Jason led them through the occupants' private living room. Somewhere in the background, Ellis heard Rossini's Seramide symphony. Not that she was in any way familiar with classical music. The only reason Ellis recognised it was because her dad had it as a ringtone for years and it used to drive her mad.

It's a little weird how it was that particular song they were hearing. She wondered where it was coming from. Were Angie and Graham around here somewhere? If so, they needed to know what was going on, if they didn't already know that is.

Her boyfriend stopped outside another door. He slowly opened it an inch, peered inside then closed it. "Shit."

"Oh God. Are the monsters in there?"

Jason shook his head. "If you mean the giant arthropods, Marty, no need to fret. It isn't them." He pulled the door open again and looked inside. "Okay," he whispered. "I need you to follow me and stay quiet! As for what's inside? It's far worse than a few giant beetles. We're about to enter the lair of their masters. The beings who control them."

CHAPTER EIGHT
SLAMMING THE GATES SHUT

If that kid of hers made another derogatory comment about his appearance, Gerald Dorset wasn't sure that he'd be able to control his actions. He slowed the red Ford and stopped a metre behind an old Ford Escort, waiting impatiently for the lights to change. Why had he actually thought that this trip would play out without incident? Ten minutes into the journey and he'd already felt like he'd swallowed a dozen large pebbles

Look at them, just look at those two little darlings in the back of that car, sitting quietly, behaving themselves and generally acting like little girls ought to. It looked like they were playing on their phones. Not that Gerald wholly approved of this insidious tech invasion but it did have its uses, on occasion.

She booted the back of his seat yet again. Of course the mother of the demon spawn hadn't seen the provocative action. The new Mrs. Dorset had her brain plugged into her tablet display. Demon spawn was no fool. The little bitch knew her game. She understood which buttons to press and when to press them. Gerald simply clamped down on his retort and gripped the wheel a little tighter. Despite the earlier promise he made to himself before his new family set off to go shopping in Bradfield's city centre, Gerald also knew how the game worked. If he even dared raise his voice to his new wife's little princess, then the eruptions really would start.

He had witnessed first-hand exactly what happened to anybody who dared to 'have a word' with Laura Dorset. The woman had gone fucking nuclear! The transformation from the ultra sexy thirty-two year old dark-haired beauty into a five foot three Tasmanian devil was scarier than the torrent of vile abuse which left her mouth. It sure did make a stark contrast to Laura and Gerald's first ever confrontation after the twelve-year-old girl poured green poster paint into his coffee cup. Now, how did that go?

"Tania does like you, Gerald. I'm sure of it. You just have to give her some time to come around, a bit of breathing space."

The lights changed. He took his foot off the brake and followed the Beetle. He passed a couple of parked police cars on the left and three more on the right. Had there been a traffic accident? Tania booted his seat again. Once again, Gerald reined in his temper, partly thanks to

Laura actually witnessing her golden child acting like the spoilt little cow that she was. He struggled to control the big smirk which threatened to explode across his face, secure in the knowledge that mummy would give Tania the biggest bollocking she had ever received. Hell, his new wife might even give the little bitch a well-earned slap!

"Please don't do that, honey. It is rather annoying."

Having uttered the barest minimum of reprimands, she plugged the earphones back in and returned to her tablet, obviously thinking those few words made her mum of the year. His eyes were too busy watching the road to check if those two exchanged secret smiles.

Several more pebbles joined the others. If this carried on, Gerald would have his own rock garden inside his ribcage.

Jesus Christ. What was wrong with the woman? Why could Laura not see how spoilt her only daughter was acting?

"Did you know that your bald patch has gone all red, Gerald? Looks dead weird, and funny. Kinda matches your fat hands."

How was it even possible for his life to have gone from fairy dust and soft rainbows to soft, stinking shit in the space of two weeks? It could only happen to him, Mr. Unlucky. To think that he believed that his string of bad luck, granted, caused by poor judgement and poor choices, was finally over.

She walked into his life. This stunning woman, beautiful and intelligent. Adored the Beetles, had no issues with him collecting scale model rally cars and, to cap it off, had a libido which even he had trouble believing.

Gerald already knew she had a young girl from a previous relationship. Hell, Laura made sure that he was cool with that even before she took Gerald back to her house. Thing is, back in the beginning, they got on great. Tania was such a lovely little girl. Polite and well-behaved. Oh, she did have her moments, the odd mood and the occasional strop when she didn't get her own way but nothing drastic. He actually believed that this was it, his own ready-made family. As the days turned into weeks, that belief never wavered, so much so that Gerald asked Laura to be his wife. She said yes straight away. Her daughter on the other hand wasn't too keen. Fuck, that was the understatement of the century.

Like daughter like mother, they say? It was certainly true with those two. Although it would be another week before he witnessed the inferno under his bride-to-be's skin, Gerald got a taster when, upon hearing the news, Tania had, what only could be described as 'a fucking meltdown'.

She kicked the back of his seat again. He didn't rise, instead he made a mental calculation and figured out he only had to put up with Laura's little bundle of joy for five years, maybe six. Tania might not even reach her eighteenth birthday before some poor bastard ended up getting the girl pregnant. Could he handle six years of low-level annoyance? He thought back to last night and the three hours of ecstasy and decided that he could indeed do the time. After all the shit that life had thrown at him ever since his mother died of cancer twenty-one years ago, surely nothing else could go wrong now.

"Look at that, Gerald. Another police car. I wonder what's going on."

They were getting close to the town centre now, and the traffic had begun to slow down. He stopped behind the Beetle and followed her gaze. Sure enough, there was yet another police car by the side of the road. Unlike the others he'd passed, this one was empty. Gerald soon discovered why. Several cars in front of the Beetle was a roadblock, staffed by three police officers as well as a couple of soldiers.

The soldiers approached the first car and gestured to the occupant to wind their window down. Two police officers walked past them and did the same to a blue van. Gerald wound his own window down and stuck his head out, trying to get a better view.

"Can you see anything?"

He shook his head. "No more than I can looking through the windscreen," replied Gerald. The car at the front of the queue turned right and vanished down a side street. He followed its progress as best he could, noticing more military personnel standing on the kerb. The blue transit soon followed the first car. The queue moved forward a few feet, giving Gerald a better view of the side street. There was yet another road block at the end, staffed by more police and soldiers. The only difference that he could make out was that the coppers over there were all decked out in body armour and carried assault weapons.

"I don't think we'll be going into town today," he muttered. When the seat kicking started up again, Gerald realised he really should have kept his prediction to himself and let either the soldiers or the police explain the situation to her. Gerald gave his wife his best pleading look but he wasted it as she wasn't even looking in his direction.

The kicking continued.

The seat buckle unlatched. Gerald wound the window back up then spun around. "For crying out loud!" he shouted. "Stop booting my fucking seat!"

He felt the slap before he saw it. Laura then grabbed his thigh and dug her nails through the thin trouser fabric and into his flesh.

"I've told you before about berating my daughter." Her voice stayed calm and flat. She might as well be discussing the weather. "I won't tell you again, Gerald. Do you understand?"

She removed her hand. He didn't need to see his skin to know she'd drawn blood. Gerald moved the car forward when another two cars were directed down the side street. He buckled himself in then wrapped his fingers tight around the wheel. His new wife and her daughter exchanged that smile. This time he saw it through the back mirror. A dozen thoughts screamed through his mind, all of them bad, all of them telling Gerald that meeting this woman and allowing her to get under his skin had been the worst decision that he had ever made.

The girl had stopped kicking the back of his seat. She now sat cross-legged, arms folded with a big smile across her face. When Tania noticed him looking through the mirror, she treated him to a big wink, followed by the middle finger. All he could do was to hang on to the steering wheel and hope the shakes would soon go.

"Please don't do that, Tania," said her mother. "It's not very nice. Now, why don't you look out of your window. Can you see that hunky soldier heading this way, honey? I want best behaviour from you, while we find out what's going on." Laura put her hand back on his thigh.

The shame he felt after involuntarily flinching at Laura's touch ran all the way down to the bone marrow. Gerald did his best to cover it up by coughing and pretending to jump but he knew full well that his crap theatrics didn't fool her.

"As for you, I don't care what rubbish is happening, we are going shopping in town." The woman's eyes flicked to the side. "Don't look at me like that, Gerald. It's probably the tremors that caused one of the buildings to become unsafe, or something. The council got all over-protective when that woman and her pram almost fell down a crack." An innocent smile suddenly appeared on her face and she pulled her top down an inch. "He's coming. Let's get this out of the way."

Even after the trauma and the revelation of knowing he was trapped between these two manipulative females, Gerald couldn't help but to find one particular part of his anatomy stirring at the sight of that radiant smile.

A single tap on the side window made him jump for real. He pulled his gaze away from those magnificent mounds, wound the window down and looked up at the sour-faced soldier. "What's going on in there?"

"It's a gas leak, sir. I need you to take the next left and go back the way you came."

After saying what he'd probably said to dozens of other motorists, the soldier took a step back, obviously thinking he'd made his instructions perfectly clear. Gerald felt her grip on his thigh tighten. Laura leaned across his knee and pushed her hand out of the window. He had spotted the soldier checking out his wife. He must have thought that Gerald had to be the luckiest bastard on the planet.

"Excuse me!" she shouted, waving him back. "We really need to go into town today. Are you really sure you can't let us through?"

He couldn't quite catch the soldier's reply. Gerald didn't need to. Her body had gone rigid. Somebody had the audacity to refuse her will. He quietly moaned, knowing full well that Laura was about to make a scene.

"You are going to do as you're fucking told. Stop grinning at me you small-dick faggot and lift that barrier before I come out there and kick your teeth in."

He moved a couple of inches, showing Gerald exactly what Laura stamping her foot had achieved. That was no gas leak. He'd served in the forces (Another bad choice) Gerald knew full well that some mild domestic emergency, or some random female screaming abuse at them would not make those lads so uneasy. He probably would have picked up the signals if he wasn't going through his own domestic emergency at the time. The soldier lifted his rifle a couple of inches. He saw fear in those eyes.

Gerald slapped her hand off the window, grabbed the woman by the shoulders and slammed her back into the seat.

"Get your fucking hands off me," she spat.

"Do you want to get shot?" Gerald employed a similar calm and placid tone she had used on him a moment ago. It appeared to work, to a degree. "I know another route into town. I guarantee that there'll be no soldiers guarding it." He quickly wound the window up, put the car in gear and followed the car that had been behind them down the side street, fully aware that the soldier continued to watch them, meaning whoever was behind this probably would not stop watching the car until it was safety away from the area.

He turned right after reaching the next roadblock, carried on driving for another half mile until Gerald passed a petrol station. All traffic on the other side leading into town had stopped and from here, it looked like the tailback stretched forever. He slowed down and turned into a side street. Gerald left the car and stretched his back while taking in a lungful of fume tainted air. He stayed still, hands on hips, with a painted smile while those two glared at him. It did occur to Gerald that he could solve all his problems by running away. Okay, so he'd lose the car and miss out on so much incredible sex but surely wasn't that a good enough price to pay to have his old, comfortable, boring life back?

Tania stuck her tongue out and he responded in kind. As he expected, the elder demon climbed out of her side, slammed the door shut then gave Gerald a look that could curdle fresh milk. He returned the glare, safe in the knowledge that his car was between them.

"What the hell are you playing at now, Gerald? Get your backside back in this fucking car right now!"

It felt so strange to hear her swearing. It kinda helped to cement what was planned for him if he didn't get as far away from these two as he could. Gerald also noticed that she used the same condescending tone as his stepmother used whenever she spoke his name. "We walk from here, Laura."

"You can think again. I'm not walking anywhere."

He shrugged. "Suit yourself. You can stay here with your demon spawn and sulk while I go into town." Gerald kept the same placid gentle tone, even though he really did want to scream his head off. "You had better remind me what you wanted again. I seem to have forgotten." The bristles vanished as quickly as they appeared. Her face, demeanour and attitude softened. He blinked a few times, unsure of how this woman had achieved such a remarkable transformation. Before his very eyes, his Mr. Hyde turned.

"I'm sorry, Gerald. I didn't mean to snap at you, it's just..." A single tear rolled down her cheek. "Well, you know how important prom night is for Tania, and Gracey's is the only shop around here that has what she wants." Laura wiped her face and gave him a radiant smile. "Friends?"

Gerald faltered. Something important had just happened and it took a few moments for it to sink in. They had just set up their first relationship boundary. Was the woman still doing her best to manipulate him, to get Gerald to do her bidding? Sure she was but even Laura must have known that she'd pushed him too far. He walked a little closer to the car, pausing before reaching for the door. He wanted to gaze upon that angelic face for another moment before hitting her with the hard truth.

"I wasn't lying about having to walk, Laura. The only way in now is through a narrow stone alley." Gerald stayed silent about the authorities clocking the car registration plate. Gerald saw the coldness descending and held out his hand as well as his best warm smile.

"Fine," she replied. "Have it your way."

Laura opened the passenger door and unbuckled her daughter. Her icy demeanour hadn't shifted but the woman was at least doing as he asked. Perhaps he didn't need to run away after all? Laura took his hand. She squeezed a little too hard and showed him her perfect teeth. Okay, so he had to face the fact that Gerald had married a demon and those milky slabs could quite easily bite off his nose but on the other hand, he had experienced what pleasures that mouth could give.

"Bite the bullet," he whispered.

"What was that?"

"Nothing. Come on, lovely ladies. It's just over the road." Gerald pulled them across the empty street while looking both ways. Not for other cars but for signs of any more police and soldiers. It had occurred to him earlier on that entering the town centre was probably the stupidest thing he could ever do considering they still had no idea why they had set up the barriers.

Laura leaned over and kissed him on the side of the neck. "Isn't this exciting?" Her fingers tickled his inside thigh. "I can't tell you how hot this is making me feel, Gerald."

He suppressed his grin. This wasn't stupid at all. It basically came down to working out which buttons to press to stop this highly-strung woman from turning his life into a waking nightmare. This situation wasn't going to happen every day, Gerald just needed to figure out something similar, a job or pastime which funnelled all of her anger and spite into sexual excitement. Paintball perhaps?

Perhaps not. Knowing Laura, she'd insist on using live ammunition and what would stop her from running away with some other younger, fitter, more handsome player? Nothing, he guessed, apart from that aforementioned imaginary love-rival would not put up with the strange and violent mother/daughter relationship that Gerald was still trying to wrap his head around.

He threaded them through the end of the alley and out into bright sunlight. Gerald had brought them into one of the many trader's courtyards in town. Most of the public never knew these places even existed, especially since the council installed security gates on most of the entrances. As his company had won the contract, he knew where they all were. Gerald also remembered the back-door combination code programmed into every gate, which, in these circumstances, would come in handy.

"It smells funny."

"This is where they dump all the rubbish, honey. That's to be expected."

"I know that, mum," replied Tania. "I'm not an idiot, you know. I mean it smells funny. It's really weird. I don't know, like hot muck or something."

As much as he hated agreeing with the brat, she did have a point. There was a peculiar taint in the air. Hot dirt was the best description he could think of, too. That's not all either. Apart from his wife's laboured breathing, Gerald failed to detect any other sound. Strange, considering they weren't that far from the road. Why couldn't he hear the traffic?

The urge to run away travelled up his body and lodged itself in his throat, it even worked free and reached Gerald's brain stem when he spotted something else which had no place in this empty yard.

Resting on top of a pile of black bin bags, at the other end of the yard, Gerald spotted a single black boot. Nothing too remarkable about that until, at least from this distance, it looked like the foot was still inside. "I think we should go back to the car," he suggested. "Something isn't right about this place."

"Mum, what is he going on about? I don't want to go back. I want, I need that dress!"

Rather than jumping into a confrontation that Gerald had no hope of winning, he simply pulled the pair towards the pile of bin bags.

"What are you doing, Gerald?"

Her mild tone betrayed an undercurrent of future emotional torment for him if he didn't explain his actions. "There is a severed foot inside that boot over there." His tone was equally mild but still loud enough for both females to hear it.

Laura let him go and marched over to the boot, while muttering under her breath. He stopped dead, watching in utter disbelief while the woman scrambled up the pile, retrieved the boot and stuck her hand inside.

"God, you are such a moron, Gerald. It's a plastic foot, you know left over from Halloween? Wait, did you really think it was real?" Her harsh laughter pummelled his ears, made even worse when the brat joined in. "Really, you get worse." She threw the boot into another alley then crouched in front of him. "I'll tell you what we'll do. Once we have Tania's dress, I'll treat you with a gift." Laura gave her daughter another knowing smile followed by a sly wink. "You know, I'm sure there's a stall in the old market where you can buy your man a new set of balls."

This prompted Tania to take up the giggling again, which stopped abruptly when the boot flew out from inside the dark alley and landed by Laura's feet. He grabbed both Laura and Tania's wrists and pulled them back while slowly backing away himself. That smell, the hot dirt odour had grown stronger.

"Who's in there?" yelled Laura. She opened her black leather purse, rummaged through the insides before her hand emerged clutching a small silver canister. "Come on, stop taking the piss. Come on out, or I swear to God that I'll come in and knock your fucking block off!"

She wrenched her wrist out of his grip and stormed forward,

gesturing to Tania to do the same. When Gerald refused to release her, Laura spun around. He found himself facing a full on attack. She held the cannister in front of her and he finally worked out what she was armed with.

"Wait, is that mace?"

"Let her go, right now, you big coward or I'll..."

Tania's sudden piercing shrieking cut her off in mid-shout. He tore his gaze from Laura and stared in utter terror and disbelief at what had emerged from the alleyway. Gerald reached for Laura only for her to blast him with the spray. Thankfully, her aim was off, so most of the pepper spray hit his cheek but some of the stuff did enter his eyes. Enough for Gerald to forget about the sight of two brown centipedes, both the length of buses, scuttling over to Laura. He forgot about Tania finally getting free, running over to her mum, only for a giant black beetle to rise out from under those bin bags, catch the girl between its huge mandibles and cut her in two. Gerald even forgot about the appearance of what could only be described as insect people. Five of them followed the centipedes out from the alleyway and headed straight towards him. He dropped to his knees, doing his best to cut out the wet noise of those monsters dining on human flesh. Gerald moaned softly, tears streaming from both eyes, while cursing himself for not being able to make the right choice in life.

"My poor decisions have made me!" he shouted. The insect men had now formed a rough semi-circle around his quivering form. Two of them lifted their stick-like forearms and he saw they held what looked suspiciously like saw-blades. A high-pitched whistling sound filled the air. "And now my poor decisions will undo me!" He screamed as instruments they held cut through his flesh like a steak knife through raw liver.

CHAPTER NINE
INNER SPACE INVADERS

It kinda encouraged Andrew to see that this shitty market had not changed much since he'd last set foot in here. Fuck knows how long that had been, probably about the same time Andrew had decided that school was for losers. He stopped next to a litter-bin, overflowing with rubbish and reloaded the shotgun. Four shots left, after that, this thing would be useless. He even doubted it would be all that effective as a club. An axe, that's what he needed, or a heavy sword. More ammo is what he really wanted but he wasn't going to find that in here.

Nelson had also stopped a few paces in front of him. "Those insect things are in here too," he hissed.

"How can you possibly know that?"

He tapped his nose. After a lifetime of being in this game, you got a feeling for it. "The lack of people is a big giveaway too, that and the severed arm lying across those books over there." He suddenly took a left and raced over to the shops lining the edge of the market. Nelson waited until Andrew caught up before continuing. "It's up to you, boss. You wanna hole up or keep moving? To be honest, I'd vote for the latter, ain't gonna find out what the fuck is going on by shivering under some bastard table."

Andrew found himself nodding, unsure of how to answer Nelson. How could the old bastard treat this damn situation so matter of factly? Like a giant insect invasion was something which happened on a daily basis? Oh sure, even before setting off, he was fully prepared to deal with the unexpected. Something was bound to go wrong during the robbery but tackling a beetle the size of a horse? Fuck no, nobody sane could or would expect anything like that.

Could that be the answer? Had the appearance of all these armour-plated monstrous killing machines finally tipped Nelson over the edge? It seemed a reasonable assumption. The old bastard had never been the most stable of characters.

"I'll take that as a yes. In that case, we'd better tool up, you know, find something a little quieter and more effective than our popguns. We ain't never gonna get to their soft bits, not through all that shell. I reckon we don't need to though. Their legs are pretty thin. A decent machete would do the trick." He nodded to himself. "Yeah, lob off a few limbs and those bastards won't be going anywhere. Be like bricking up a car, I guess."

57

"Nelson, you are aware of where we are? I mean, look around you, man. This place sells samosas, batteries, crap Chinese made toys and mobile phones. It's not exactly known for selling offensive weapons."

His colleague laughed at him. "Man, you really are a funny guy. You know that? Who said anything about picking what we need off the shelf? Come on, follow me." Nelson hurried past two clothing shops, a jewellers, a shop selling Eastern European food and stopped outside a shuttered up electronics shop. "What we need to level the playing field will be in here."

"Nelson, it's locked up, man." What was this idiot playing at? It seemed like a dumb time to start looking for another knock-off mobile phone. "More to the point, Nelson, this place ain't gonna sell what we need."

"Remember what I said about not picking off the shelf? Look, I knew this guy in block 8 who knew this other fella who told him all about how some of these market traders use these shops as a front. Well, I did some extra digging after you approached me with your little scheme." He bent over and examined the lock on the bottom right, then looked at the other one on the opposite side.

"Great, so how do you know which shop is the dodgy one?"

Nelson tapped his nose again. "Told you, it's a knack." He passed Andrew his gun. "Best you do what you do best and keep us from getting eaten."

"Wait, say what?"

He pulled out a small brown leather rolled up sheet and laid it out by his knee. It contained a variety of thin metal picks. "We're being followed. Also, that severed arm vanished the moment we passed it. I reckon there's only one out there, maybe two. Still, I would appreciate not dying while I work on these locks, you know?"

He thrust the gun into his waistband then stepped away from the shop, and leaned against a concrete pillar. Andrew still wasn't all that convinced about being followed. He hadn't heard anything and his hearing was keener than Nelson's that's for sure. The only sound that reached his ears came from the scratching noise made by the old man's metal picks. Andrew then held his breath and closed his eyes just for a moment. That really was the only noise he could pick up, like the whole market was sound-proofed or something.

There wasn't anything following them. Apart from him, nothing moved. The old guy was obviously losing it. Still, just to be sure, Andrew decided to have a quick scout along both directions, just to see if there really was anything lurking up those paths between the stalls. He shouldered the shotgun and ran back towards the bank, staying close to the market edge shops, while looking up every aisle. It took him less than thirty seconds and saw absolutely fuck all. It must be true. Nelson really was losing it.

Andrew slowly walked back to his mate, not really seeing any point in checking the other direction. Even from here, it looked clear enough. He had no idea why Nelson had gotten all nervous in the first place. Maybe his conscience was having a go at him for shooting that bank employee? Even to Andrew, the old man's behaviour was a bit out of place. Like that poor bastard was in any fit state to pick Nelson out of an identity parade. Like anyone was even going to realise that his gang had robbed that bank!

That made him stop. Why had they told Tony to go wait in the sodding car? They knew what was happening. Well, they didn't but all three men had known something seriously fucked up had gone down. Having someone to watch his back while Nelson did what he did best would have been so much easier. He sighed heavily. Not that Andrew needed anyone right now. This market was quieter than a fucking tomb.

He wondered how the kid was coping out there. Hell, Andrew didn't even know if Tony was still alive. He didn't even know if the poor bastard had managed to get back to the car without one of those monsters getting to him first.

Tony would be alright, he was a tough kid. Andrew needed to worry more about his predicament, even if, at the moment, he was in no apparent danger. That started to niggle him. Not the no danger bit, although that did play a part, it was the lack of sound which worried him. Even if the insects had raided the market, there should still be some noise. No music, no mobile phones going off, no moaning, no nothing, apart from the ever present scratching sound.

Andrew's heart beat a little faster. There's no way that he ought to be able to hear Nelson trying to pick that lock! Not from here. What else could it be? He hadn't seen anything moving in here. Andrew hugged the gun a little tighter and slowly made his way back to Nelson, aware that the scratching noise continued. He jerked to a halt when Andrew saw Nelson. The old man stood with his back flattened against the shutter. He looked terrified.

Nelson urgently shook his head then rolled his eyes towards the ceiling. Andrew lifted his head. Three huge black beetles stared back at him. They clung to the old ventilation ducts which stretched across the entire market. The noise he could hear came from those things rubbing their back legs against their outer shell.

One of the beetles scurried upwards and vanished into the blackness. The remaining creatures moved at lightning speed to the edge of the wall, then stopped. He tore his gaze off them and followed the path of that duct until he reached one of the openings. It looked wet around the edge. His stomach swirled when the realisation dawned as to why they hadn't found any people. Those things must have killed them and dragged their bodies up there and stuffed them inside the ducts.

At least, he hoped to fuck that they were dead. Andrew remembered reading something about how some insects just stun their prey then lay eggs inside their bodies. Those eggs hatched as the babies ate their way out. Andrew raised his gun. There's no way he was going to let that happen to him!

"Lower the gun, man!" hissed Nelson. "That's only going to piss them off. Besides, I think there's more than three up there."

He kept the gun trained on those monsters and took one careful step towards the shop. "Is that shutter still locked?"

Nelson nodded.

"Fuck. Any bright ideas?" Both beetles scurried halfway down the wall. "Into the arcade!" yelled Andrew. He took aim and squeezed off one shot. The blast hit the wall between the monsters, shredding four of their legs. Both beetles fell and landed a few feet in front of the two men. They scurried in a circle, smashing into each other before rushing to the left and vanishing into the market interior.

The danger was far from over. The noise from the blast had opened a deluge of sounds. Some familiar, some not so recognisable. Over the ringing in his ears, Andrew could now make out the sound of moaning, of soft weeping, as well as cries for help. They were coming from all around them. Some were, as he feared, drifting down from the inside of those ventilation ducts. Human misery wasn't all he heard. The sounds he couldn't hear before now made themselves known. From somewhere inside the market, Andrew could make out the theme tune from an old 80's Saturday teatime TV show. What he heard more than anything else was the clicking. Lots and lots of clicking. He looked up and discovered Nelson was indeed right. The ceiling was alive with dozens of those giant monsters!

"Stop gawping, you fool!" snapped Nelson. The old man grabbed Andrew's collar and pulled him into the next shop. He pulled the pistol out of Andrew's waistband then ran through the middle of the arcade and stopped beside a change machine. "Forget the machete idea, we need a few grenades."

Andrew caught up with him, keeping his gaze on the opening while expecting those things to flood the place at any second. There was no way that their pitiful weapons would keep them at bay for more than a few seconds. They'd be better off getting it over and done with by turning the fund on themselves. He waited, hardly daring to breathe, unable to take his eyes away from the shop entrance. At either side, the machines showed off their retro graphic displays, encouraging whoever passed them to swap coins for a few minutes of pleasure.

The seconds stretched into an eternity. Beside him, Nelson's rapid breathing fought against Andrew's excitable heart for dominance. He moved a little closer to the counter and rested his aching arm on the glass top. Why hadn't they entered? He saw first-hand how fast they could move. By rights, the pair of them should be ankle deep in insect gore about now, almost out of ammo and totally out of options.

"Do you think they might have forgotten about us?"

Nelson's sudden whisper scared the hell out of him. "How should I know. Why don't you go have a look? Maybe give them a little wave?"

"Fuck off, Andrew. I'm serious. We shouldn't still be alive."

"Yeah, I know that," replied Andrew. He moved backwards, further inside the arcade. "Come on. Let's make ourselves scarce and not invite a confrontation. At least get under cover and away from the entrance."

He counted to five then turned and raced down the middle, running past several sit-down racing games, noting fresh blood on at least two of the black plastic seats. So the monsters had already been in here and fed. He had to stop. Andrew grabbed the side of one of the cabinets and scrunched up his eyes and winced at the image he'd just received.

He saw himself sitting in this very machine, feeding in another pound coin. He felt a little uneasy, sure that somebody in the distance had just screamed. Must be his imagination or some kids having a joke. It had nothing to do with him.

Just another thirty thousand to go to knock off those hateful initials of ORC from the top slot in the high score table. All the others belonged to him or that thirty-something skinny guy who spent every Wednesday afternoon in the arcade.

He heard another scream just when the continue hit 5. It was nothing to do with him. He pressed the continue button and was immediately back into the action. Several waves of attack fighters emerged from behind a large asteroid but he was ready for them and vaporised them with his last plasma bomb. The end of level guardian was just ahead but first he had to...

Three more screams took him out of the game. Several kids ran past his cabinet on both sides. The screaming grew more intense. He leaned out of the cabinet and saw nothing but crowds of people desperate to get out of the arcade. He then made the mistake of looking over his shoulder. He couldn't help but join in with the screaming. Hot piss ran down his legs but he was hardly aware. What the fuck was that thing sliding down the stairs, what the fuck was it? Oh no. Oh fuck. It had seen him. It was coming straight for...

Andrew snapped open his eyes. "What the fuck just happened to me?" he gasped.

"Hey, are you okay, man? You've gone as white as a sheet."

He turned his head and allowed his eyes to refocus before answering. "I think I just saw some kid die. Like, you know, in a vision or something."

"Are you winding me up?"

"Of course I'm not winding you up." Andrew peered inside the cabinet. The game was the same. It waited a moment until the high score table was displayed. Sure enough, there it was, right at the top of the score table, the name which that kid had been so desperate to beat, ORC. Andrew spotted a patch of thick blood on the seat and backed out, feeling a little nauseous. "Christ. I don't know what just happened. One second I was standing right here, feeling dizzy, the next, I was in this kid's head, playing the game when the insects turned up and started eating people."

"Right, and these beetles ate this kid?"

Andrew shook his head again. "No, this is where it gets really fucking kooky. It wasn't any kind of giant insect that we've already seen. I mean, they were insects but these guys kinda looked, I don't know. They looked like humanoid insects. One of these things came down those steps right behind you and..." he shook his head. "Can't remember. Killed him, I guess."

"You are aware of how mad that just sounded?"

"Of course I am. I'm not an idiot. Saying that, is it any more mad than being attacked by a giant beetle?"

"Yeah, I know, but, come on, man. Fucking insect people?"

"Look, forget it. Come on, let's see where those steps lead."

Nelson looked back over to the entrance before he took the steps two at a time. Andrew followed but he took his time, still trying to wrap his head over what he had just experienced. He reached the top and leaned over the metal railing. From this vantage he could see the mess made when those giant insects raided the arcade. Christ. Those poor bastards never stood a chance. It looked like a slaughterhouse floor.

"Andrew have you got a minute?"

He turned and moved away from the railing. Nelson stood in front of a gap between two slot machines. "What have you found?" it was the old man's turn to look pale. Hell, the guy was positively fucking transparent.

"This kid. You know, the one whose head you magically jumped into. I don't suppose you can remember what he was wearing by any chance?"

"What?" Andrew closed his eyes. "Wait on, he had this scruffy dark brown jacket and a pair of grimy jeans. Oh, he had a baseball cap on too. Come on, what is this about?"

"You had better come here, man."

He approached Nelson, curious as well as a little fearful as to what he might have stumbled across. Andrew saw it before reaching the old man. It hung on a wet, light brown, smooth cord, as thick as his wrist. It looked, for want of another word, like some giant chrysalis. He kinda doubted that a beautiful butterfly was going to emerge from this though. Andrew stepped a little closer, then stopped dead when he found what it contained. "Oh no. Fucking hell, it's him! That's the kid. The poor bastard, what's happening to him?"

The clothes were the same, as were the general shape and mass of the body, but everything else remotely human no longer existed. At least, not that Andrew could make out. A dark, bark-like substance covered all the visible skin and hundreds of thread-like vines covered the new growth. He leaned a little closer. "Okay, this is seriously freaking me out." He turned his head. "I don't even want to know what is happening in there."

Andrew stood up and reached for his blade. "That poor kid." He was almost ready to slice through that cord when Nelson grabbed his wrist.

"What the fuck are you playing at, man?"

"What does it look like? I can't allow that kid to suffer. It's fucking inhumane."

Nelson kept hold of Andrew's arm. "Look, man. I sympathise, I really do. I mean you two obviously shared a moment or something, but you have no idea what cutting that cord could do."

"Will you get off me already?"

The old man shook his head. "Fuck no. Have you not worked out how we can possibly still be breathing? Come on, Andrew think it through. Why did those monsters not follow us into the arcade?"

He loosened his grip and the knife clattered to the floor. "You think they were protecting this?"

Nelson bent down, retrieved the knife and handed it back to Andrew. "No, not them. Maybe your insect people. I mean, I doubt this is the only chrysalis thing in this arcade. Makes sense that they'll want to protect them, but not with your heavy artillery."

"Are you buying into this intelligent insect thing now?" Andrew put away the knife. It then hit him exactly what Nelson had just said. "Heavy artillery?"

Nelson nodded. "Sure, why not. Living tanks, and you ain't going to use such massive animals to protect such delicate devices. Oh no, you're going to use something much smaller, something which ain't going to steam-roll over all your valuable gear."

Andrew was not slow on the uptake. He knew exactly what Nelson was suggesting. "Guardian insects, you mean."

"Yeah, fucking guardian insects and we've both fallen inside a shitty science fiction movie. Only the stakes are our lives."

"Ain't great odds either. Come on, let's see if we can find a way out of your movie without ending up as dinner."

"Or inside a chrysalis."

"Yeah. That too." Andrew took the lead, he made his way past another bank of slot machines, looking everywhere, including up, to see if anything really was watching them. There were a couple of moments when he swore something up in the shadows moved but that could have been down to nerves and his imagination. After all, if they were being watched then surely these guardians would kill him and Nelson just out of general principle? Had they not already proven themselves capable of doing harm to their precious jewel? He paused beside an ancient pinball machine.

"Andrew, what's wrong?"

He moved to one side.

"Holy fuck!" exclaimed Nelson.

More cocoons filled the space between the back wall and the pinball machine. All identical to the one they had passed earlier. Andrew stopped counting when he reached thirty. "God, these things really stink." Andrew slowly walked past the pinball machine and stopped next to one of the outer chrysalises. He avoided all temptation to peer inside, not wanting to find out what kind of damage the stuff had already caused to the poor sod inside, instead he did his best to look past all these unholy things and stare at the wall. Did something over there just blink?

"Wait, hang on, where are you going now?"

"I thought I saw a green light on that wall, Nelson."

"So what?"

Andrew didn't bother answering him, instead he pushed through the hanging bodies, wincing at the feel of the hard outer casing. It was warm, a little sticky and all together totally unpleasant. When caterpillars entered these things, the forces inside literally rewrote their DNA. If the same was happening to these people, what was going to be the finished article? Was he looking at the birth of more insect people, like the ones he saw in his vision?

"Oh, of course," said Nelson. "I can't believe I've been so thick."

The old man had finally got it. Andrew reached the end of the cocoons and wiped slime on his pants while staring at the green fire exit sign above his head. "I think it's time to get the fuck out of here." He slammed the bar down and pushed open the door, unprepared for the eye-watering bright light which flooded the dim room.

"Breathe that in, man," said Nelson. "So that's what fresh air smells like. Come on, let's make tracks. Tony is going to be wondering where we are."

It was Andrew's turn to stop someone from making a life changing mistake. "Hold your horses for a second," he said, grabbing Nelson's arm. "Something isn't right." His eyes had already adjusted to the bright sunlight and although the town looked quiet enough, the immediate area below the metal stairs was full of shiny white bones. He leaned out and looked up towards the felt roof, just as another bone fell off and plummeted down. There was movement up there! Andrew spotted a grey trainer lying on the first step. He ran out, scooped it up and hurried back to Nelson.

"What are you playing at?"

"Hush your lips. Just watch." Andrew threw the shoe as hard as he could. It didn't even get past the edge of the metal fire escape before something plucked it out of the air. The thing which snatched it looked like a wasp, only a hundred times bigger and painted black and red. It dropped the shoe, spun around in mid-air then flew straight for them!

"Holy fuck!" Andrew pulled Nelson back inside. He grabbed the bar but it was too late. The huge predator had already curled three of its legs around the door edge. Its strength was phenomenal. Despite using all his strength on that bar, the giant creature easily pulled the door out of his grasp. If Nelson hadn't been holding on to his belt, it's possible that Andrew could have found himself flying over the edge of the gantry and smashing into the ground. That is, if another one of those wasp things appeared and grabbed him.

The monster rushed them again. Nelson threw him to the floor before dropping to one knee. The old man already had the pistol in his hands. He got off two shots. The first one clipped its wings while the last shot blew off the monster's head.

Andrew rolled to the side then jumped up and ran back to the wide open fire-door. The serene landscape no longer existed. There were monsters everywhere. Three more giant wasps had dropped from the roof and were now clinging to the side of the brick wall. He saw several beetles, of different shapes, colours and sizes, all scuttling towards the bottom of the gantry. Andrew also spotted his first real sighting of the insect-men. Two of the things stood on the roof of a black delivery van. He quickly grabbed the bar and pulled it shut. It was obvious that they weren't escaping by this route.

He stood with his back against the wall, sweat dripping off his face. Nelson stood motionless close to the downed monster. The room was not silent. A quiet muffled screaming was leaking from one of the cocoons close to where Nelson stood. It took him a few moments to work out why. The old man's first shot hadn't just clipped the monster's wing, it had continued its trajectory and punctured a chrysalis. Thick red and yellow fluid ran down its casing and dripped onto the floor to form an uneven puddle. Andrew reckoned that if any of these insect guardians were going to show then this would be the opportune moment.

"I'm guessing we're not leaving through the fire door?"

The screaming had stopped now. He offered up a short prayer for the life that Nelson's stray bullet had cut short, thinking that at least the soul inside the casing died while still being human. Nothing had rushed in to investigate so perhaps the old man's theory of guardian insects was invalid? If so, then did they have a duty to put bullets into the rest of these dirty things?

"Andrew, are you still there?"

"Yeah, sorry. I was wool-gathering."

"You picked a good time to do that."

"There's no way we can leave that way. The courtyard is swarming with giant insects. We wouldn't last ten seconds." He decided not to mention the insect men. "We have to find another way out."

It took Nelson a few seconds before replying. "Teleport?"

"What?" The old man simply shook his head then started to push his way through the hanging cocoons.

"Hey, where are you going?" Andrew ran after him. He finally caught up with the old man just as he reached the pinball machine. Nelson stood next to it. His pistol was pointing straight at Andrew's face. "What's this, man?"

Nelson shrugged. "Guess you weren't the only one who was wool-gathering. Thing is, the way I see it. we need to face the simple fact that we are out of options. I guess utterly fucked would be a more precise way of putting it. We're not going to get out of this place alive." Nelson paused. His tongue ran along his bottom lip. "At least one of us isn't."

66

"Right, and you think what? That offering me up to the monsters will buy you enough time to escape?" Andrew was too tired and sick of this shit to even pretend to feel betrayed. Hell, he wasn't even all that scared. Not that he didn't think Nelson would go through with his insinuation. The old man's moral centre had come from Satan.

"Lay the shotgun on the floor and kick it over."

"Like that's gonna fucking happen," he yelled. "Suck my dick, you fucking turncoat."

"I'm sorry that you feel like that, old friend." He took aim.

Andrew dropped down and rolled back into the midst of the cocoons. Two shots rang out. One of them nicked his thigh. He ground his teeth to stop himself from crying out. God, that really hurt! Warm blood soaked into his pants. Nelson cursed but he didn't fire again. Instead, he pushed his way through the hanging bodies. Andrew rolled to the left. He knew escape was pointless as the wet blood he left on the floor told the old bastard exactly where he was going. "Fuck this," he muttered. Andrew managed to sit up. He aimed at the chrysalis above him and paused until Nelson stood behind it. He then fired. The shot blew him back but it also obliterated the top of the cocoon as well as taking out most of Nelson's face.

His partner in crime lay sprawled on the floor in a lake of blood mixed with the lumpy, stinking contents from the cocoon. What remained of the casing had fallen over Nelson's ankles. Amazingly, the old man still lived. Both his arms moved through the gloop. It looked like he was trying to fly. Andrew used the shotgun to help himself up, moved closer to the other man, bent down and grabbed the pistol. He was so tempted to put him out of his misery, to finish the job, but that idea went out of the window when his thigh wound gave him a timely reminder. No, fuck him. Let the untrustworthy bellend stay there, making his snow angels in the foul smelling mess. Something was bound to come along to turn the bastard into kebab meat and Andrew fully intended to be somewhere else when that happened.

He limped back towards the single chrysalis. Killing Nelson was the last thing Andrew had wanted to do but what other option did he have? The old man had practically signed his own death warrant. He had known Nelson a long time. Long enough for Andrew to understand that the stubborn bastard would not change his mind.

"Fucking marvellous. Thanks for that, Nelson," he growled. The situation hadn't changed, except for the little fact that there was nobody to watch his back. "Now what am I going to do?" Andrew hurried past the lone chrysalis without looking at it, reaching the railing and leaned over. His heart sank when he saw huge moving shadows as well as the occasional glimpse of insect leg and wing by the entrance. He turned his head and almost dropped the shotgun. "You have got to be shitting me!" The kid, the one who was supposed to be all wrapped up and turning into Christ knows what was sat inside that arcade cabinet with his hands gripping that steering wheel. "No, no way!" Andrew spun around and...

"Seriously, dude. It's a piece of piss to get out."

Andrew blinked several times. He was now leaning against the cabinet. The pain in his leg had gone and so had the weapons. "How did I get here?"

"Bollocks. That's another pound wasted." The kid stuck his head out of the side of the cabinet. "I'm not used to an audience. That's probably why I buggered up." He grinned. "Nerves, I guess. Don't fret about the moving. You're not really here. Neither am I for that matter. Kinda makes me wonder why I got so pissed at losing again. The moving bit? Oh, The Mantil call it Projection. They do it all the time apparently. Never mind about all that, dude."

"I might not have a gun but I can still punch you into next week. One last time, you annoying little turd. What the fuck is happening to me?"

The kid climbed out of the cabinet. "You were right about this place being protected. If you want to get out of here then you need to give them a reason to protect you too, dude." He nodded over to the shadows just outside the entrance. "Figure it out."

He was back beside the railing. "Figure it out? What the hell is that supposed to mean? Figure what out?" Andrew turned and marched right up to the chrysalis. "I need more than that, you geeky little twat." He jerked and swung his gun around, believing that something was right beside him but the only movement he saw was Nelson, still wriggling about in the muck. Andrew watched him for a moment before moving a little closer to the severely wounded man. He had an idea.

Andrew leaned the shotgun against the pinball machine then grabbed the old man's ankle and dragged his body closer to the railing. Thanks to the huge amount of mess under him, the job wasn't too difficult: the stuff acted as a lubricant. Once he got the body to where he wanted it, he wrapped his fingers around the man's upper arms and pulled him up. It was then just a matter of tipping him over the edge after that. Andrew slid his chest along the top of the railing then grabbed his leg again and lifted. The old man's body balanced for a couple of seconds before gravity took hold and he dropped on to the ground floor, landing in the middle of the aisle with a sickening thud.

Three beetles and a centipede rushed inside but before they could even get to the meat, hundreds of fist-sized dark-orange bugs dropped out of the ceiling and started attacking the huge intruders. Andrew swallowed hard. He picked up the shotgun and ran as fast as he could down the stairs and towards the entrance, making sure to stay well away from the carnage happening in the middle of the arcade.

CHAPTER TEN
THE SECRET GETS OUT

Jason hadn't said a single word in ten minutes now. None of the others had either. Her boyfriend explained how important it was for any of them not to make a sound. He said that all their lives depended on it. Ellis stopped walking. She leaned against the rough stone and thrust her hands deep into her pockets.

"What the hell are you doing?" hissed Lorraine.

Ellis put her finger against her mouth while continuing to look at the stone wall. As expected, the older woman squeezed past her and raced after Jason. Marty said nothing. He just gave Ellis a quizzical look before joining her. The walls were giving off heat. It hadn't been too noticeable while they'd been traversing this route but now that she'd stopped, Ellis could definitely feel the difference. She didn't even bother asking herself why. Her mind had already burst with the vast amount of unanswered questions that had smacked into her since leaving work.

"Are you okay, honey?"

She shook her head. "No, Marty. I'm far from okay." Ellis gazed at the older man. "I feel like I've fallen down the rabbit hole."

He let out a long-drawn-out breath. "I'm not far behind you there."

"Ellis, have you hurt yourself?"

Her boyfriend had come back. He stood beside her, his face a picture of concern. Jason honestly looked like he cared about her safety. Yet, after all the tiny pieces of information that he'd casually dropped whilst in that bar, Ellis just didn't know if this man, the one whom she thought she knew, was telling the truth. She turned her head, fearing that if he continued to pull that face, Ellis would either fall into his arms and burst into tears or punch the bastard in the face.

"We're almost there. Just another few metres to go and then we really will be safe. I promise you." Jason slid his fingers into hers. "Please, just give it another couple of minutes. That's all I'm asking."

Ellis couldn't stay here, sulking like some big kid, that much she did know. "Fine, have it your way," she whispered.

He grinned his famous grin and gently pulled her along with Marty following behind. Where had Lorraine gone? The woman hadn't come back with Jason after grassing on her. Was she ashamed to show her face? Thing is, Ellis didn't really know any of the people in her group, who knew what could be going through the older woman's head right now? For all Ellis knew, what was happening right here in her crappy town might be happening everywhere else. This could really be it, the End of Days, the Apocalypse. Giant insects will once again rule the land just like they did all those millions of years ago.

Did that sneaky cow have designs on Jason? Sowing the seeds of discontent while still pretending to be best of pals? Why not? If this truly was the beginning of the end then Ellis wouldn't put it past Lorraine to try to bag the alpha male. Ellis guessed that if she was in Lorraine's position, she'd probably be thinking along the same lines. Marty was a lovely man but he couldn't protect them: a warrior, Marty was not. Hell, he'd have trouble fighting his way out of a wet paper bag.

On the other hand, her over-active imagination could be just reacting really badly to her admittedly dire looking situation and feeding her mind with any old paranoid bullshit. More than likely, her friend was only looking out for her and had no intentions of stealing Jason.

Jason came to a halt. Ellis almost bumped into him, she was so consumed in her private delusional fantasy to notice that Jason's promise of a couple of minutes had already arrived. She found Lorraine too, she stood beside a perfectly ordinary panelled, polished wooden door in the same style as the bar they left. It did look a bit out of place in this stark environment.

"Are you going to explain all this secret agent stuff to us now, Jason? " asked Marty. "After all, you did promise."

"Almost ready!" he replied. "This is going to knock your socks off."

He sounded like an excitable kid getting ready to unwrap his Christmas presents or show his girlfriend what was going to be the market's newest toy stall. Was that even going to happen or was that just part of his elaborate cover? Come to think of it, was she part of Jason's cover too? If that turned out to be the case then Ellis really would knock his fucking block off.

Jason opened the door and hushed them all inside. "Welcome to the outer fringes of Geocorp Energy Solutions."

"I've heard of them," said Marty. "They had an office in town a few months ago, I remember walking past the place a couple of times. If I remember correctly, they were proposing an alternative method of producing electricity with geothermal energy. To be honest, it sounded like a con."

"No con, Marty. These guys knew their beans alright. Hell, this was their third site. Everything was going great until..." He stopped speaking for a second when they reached another door. "...They encountered what they described as an anomaly." Jason keyed in a number sequence into a keypad beside the door. "You know what? I think my CO would be better filling you in. Major Yates is such a lovely chap. You'll get on with him like a house on fire, Lorraine. He shares your evil sense of humour." The door slowly opened outwards. "Of course, we evacuated the base. There's only military..." Jason stopped again.

"Oh no," he gasped. "Wait here."

Jason ran inside. Ellis tried to follow only for Lorraine to grab her arm and pull her back.

"Honey. You heard what he said."

She was about to say something that Ellis might regret later on when Marty gave her that look and shook his head.

"Best you stay," he said. "Oh heavens. I can already smell the slaughter!"

Ellis took advantage of Lorraine's momentary distracted lapse and shook herself free then ran for the open door before the other woman could catch her. The way she saw it, Jason had the gun. Even if her boyfriend had just walked into a shit load of trouble, he'd still do everything he could to protect her. She ought to be ashamed of having such a selfish attitude. After all, looking out for number one is exactly what Ellis accused her imaginary rendition of Lorraine of doing.

She ran back to Lorraine and grabbed the woman, then dragged her towards the door "You're right, Lorraine. We ought to stick together." She glared at Marty. "All of us."

As soon as Ellis crossed the threshold, she immediately wished she had stayed on the other side of that door. "Good God!" Ellis slammed a hand over her mouth, honesty believing she was about to throw up.

"We need to get her out of here!"

Lorraine tried to pull Ellis back outside, helped by Marty, but she shook her head and stood her ground. "It's alright," she replied, looking at her friend to avoid staring at the slaughter all around the room. "Remember what I said about sticking together? This place obviously isn't as safe as Jason first believed." Ellis gave Lorraine's hand a comforting squeeze then let go and slowly, watching her steps, made her way towards Jason.

Bits of human flesh, pieces of splintered bone as well as shredded blood-stained fabric carpeted the once white-tiled floor. Ellis felt sick. She also needed to cry for the loss of all the people which must have felt more terror than any human should experience during the last moments of their lives. Ellis could only hope that their deaths were mercifully quick.

She stopped in the centre of the room and forced herself to take her eyes off the floor and look around. The tears which she'd done so well to hold back suddenly burst when Ellis noticed the signs on the walls. Oh Christ. How was this place any different from the damn factory? There they were, just the same as in her workplace, no doubt duplicated thousands of times in other work areas around the country. The no smoking signs, employee of the month awards, directions to the senior management offices and to the staff restaurant. She looked a bit closer to her position and spotted a couple of work terminals, personalised with small fluffy toys, postcards and photographs.

Those soldiers must have been quite insistent on getting everyone out of here for the people to leave all their gear behind. Unless the employees thought they were coming back. Ellis saw where the soldiers' bullets had torn into the walls now and wondered if her reaction to this slaughter would have been any different if all this torn up meat had belonged to the workers instead of the men sent in to replace them. At least the soldiers were armed, not that it did them any good.

Strange how she hadn't seen any bits of giant insect in amongst all this devastation. No piece of shell casing, no shot off leg. Nothing at all to show exactly what these guys had been fighting. Surely, at least one of the soldiers had made a kill? Unless, unless they hadn't been fighting the giant insects? Ellis went very cold.

Jason was by another terminal further inside the room. This one had no personalised gimmicks stuck around it so Ellis guessed that piece of equipment had arrived with the military. He was frantically tapping keys while staring at the monitor, looking both scared and furious. Jason finally slammed his fist into the keyboard before storming towards Ellis.

He embraced her. "I'm sorry."

"For what?"

"For bringing you here, for exposing you to this terrible danger. Mainly, I guess, for not telling you what I really did. Even if I wasn't supposed to."

"No time like the present," she replied.

He nodded, released her then looked over her shoulder. "Okay, I guess explanations are way overdue. Wait here a second while I grab the others."

Jason ran over to the door, slammed it shut then came back, tapping Marty and Lorraine on the shoulder as he passed them. They had not been idle. The pair had found an assortment of weapons in a pile on the floor. Ellis frowned and wondered if she was the only one in here who thought that if something had broken in here and started killing them, wouldn't the guns be scattered around the floor, covered in blood and gore? They wouldn't be left in a pile unless... She moaned quietly. Unless whatever had done all this had somehow managed to suppress most of them before any soldier had figured what was happening?

In her mind's eye, she pictured a couple of insects about the size of a large rat, scurrying between the rows of sleeping soldiers, stopping beside each one, biting into their bodies and injecting some kind of paralysing poison before moving onto their next victim.

Bloody hell. Ellis believed she might never sleep again now. She, once again, cursed her over-active imagination. Jason had hurried back to the pair, pulled some kind of assault weapon out of their hands then furnished them each with a pistol. He picked one of the assault weapons, a couple of magazines then hurried back to Ellis.

"Come on, guys. I think we need to get out of this place before we do anything."

"You know what happened in here," said Marty. "Don't you dare deny it either. I saw you by the computer. Were you reviewing the camera footage?"

Jason sighed. "Please, guys. Not in here. Come on, this way." He ran over to the terminal, waited for them to catch up before entering a selection of numbers into the keyboard. Moments later, a hidden door located beside a filing cabinet opened. Ellis wondered how he would have done that if he'd broken the keyboard earlier. She also was curious to know why this room had a secret door in the first place. Somehow, Ellis doubted that the military had installed it.

She and the others trooped out of the building and into a cleaner area, with cold air-conditioning getting rid of the stink which followed them inside. Even so, Ellis could still smell it on their clothes and in their hair. That wasn't the only reminder. The other three trailed bloody footprints and she suspected that her shoes were doing the same.

"I don't think they got into here," muttered Jason. "Thank God for that."

"Who are they?" shouted Marty. "Come on tell us what the fuck is happening!"

Ellis didn't know what was more shocking. Listening to the normally mild-mannered chap lose his rag or him actually swear. She looked around the featureless grey walls, noting there were another two doors on the other side of the room. The only other furnishing in here was a polished wooden boardroom table and six chairs situated around it. Laptops faced the six chairs, all were closed. Apart from the computers, the only other item on the table was a large glass ball with the company logo etched into the top. Ellis also noted that she was indeed leaving bloody footprints on the white tiled floor.

"I'm sorry, Marty. Okay, so our team was called in about two months ago when the company's drills broke through the rock face and discovered something that should not be there. Another cavern but this wasn't natural."

Three months. That's how long Jason had been seeing her.

"They tried to cover it up at first. Not surprising really, not considering how much money was at stake. Thing is, one certain board member had the decency to ask for help. Granted, the first report we did receive from this unknown individual was vague in the extreme but the images which accompanied the file sure made up for it. Of course, the powers that be thought it was a joke, I mean, it had to be a joke, either that, or someone was playing a very elaborate prank on us." Jason looked around the group, making eye contact with nobody until, that is, he reached Marty. "The company had unwittingly stumbled into the domain of another sentient race of beings. An insectoid creature who wanted nothing more than peace with our kind."

"They have a real funny way of showing it!" snapped Marty.

Jason opened one of the doors and stepped through. Ellis hurried after him. The change in scenery couldn't be any more extreme. Gone were the grey featureless walls. It looked like her boyfriend had transported them all into the bowels of the planet. She turned around, utterly gobsmacked. How was this even possible? The cavern ceiling had to be at least a hundred stories above them. It looked like they had travelled deep underground yet, as far as she knew, they were still on the surface. An optical illusion maybe, or perhaps a projection of some kind? The rough rock wall beside her glowed red. It kinda reminded Ellis of the old fire her pretend parents had in their living room back when she was a kid. She reached out, then stopped.

"It's okay," said Jason. "It's not hot. This is what they use as their light source."

Marty and Lorraine had followed them in. Lorraine spoke first. "This is unbelievable."

"They call themselves the Deltin. They really are peaceful, wanting nothing more than to exist in harmony with the other beings who share their world. They offered to show us humans, who they called the Younglings, the methods to develop the technology which their race now took for granted. Tech which they developed long before our species even evolved. The stuff they showed us made the military technical officers we brought with us wet their pants."

"Such as?"

"You have already experienced it, Marty. Look around you, We're no longer in Kansas. We are now thirty miles below the Earth's surface. Instant matter relocation." Jason tapped the cavern wall. "This is the place the company inadvertently stumbled into. Quite a find, don't you think?" He walked back to them and stopped in front of a stone archway. "This is it, at least it's one of their portal devices. Thing is, it really was dumb luck that the drills were able to hit the sweet spot. One of our techs actually calculated that the chances of this actually happening were something like one in three billion."

"Dumb luck?" replied Ellis. "Hundreds of people have died, Jason, and more will be dying unless we sort this mess out. As for your friendly insects giving us all this tech? I bet there is a catch. There always is."

Jason nodded. "Yeah, there's a catch alright. The Deltins are not the only insectoid sentient creature inhabiting these subterranean kingdoms. There's another species, a highly intelligent and hyper-aggressive race of creatures who they call the Mantil. Apparently, the two have been fighting each other for millennia." Jason sighed. "So yeah, there was a catch alright. They told us that their sworn enemy would pose no problem to us as they were on the other side of the planet and the Mantil had no idea that the planet's surface was even occupied."

Ellis had trouble digesting any of what he had spouted. It all seemed just too ridiculous for words, like a story from one of those Saturday morning cartoon shows. She closed her eyes and leaned back against the wall, allowing his words to flow over her while doing her best to pretend that none of this was really happening. Wouldn't it be nice if that was true, that she and Jason were sat in the café in the market and eating samosas, smothered in chilli sauce? A portion of hot chips on the side for afters. Yeah, that sounded ideal. Aroon would be in the background, chatting up somebody else this time, while his dad looked on in disapproval. There'd be no tremors in this fantasy, no holes in the ground and definitely no fucking huge bugs. What would her hunky boyfriend be doing? Talking, of course, probably about toys. He'd be excitedly explaining to her his latest obsession, a rare toy line based on a cartoon where giant insects and their insectoid masters fought for dominance over a shattered planet long after the human race became extinct. Ellis snapped open her eyes. "For crying out loud," she whispered. What was wrong with her brain? That was even worse than reality!

It took Ellis a moment to realise that nobody was speaking any more. She pulled her head away from the wall, leaned forward and instinctively pushed a fist in her mouth to stop the scream from blasting out.

"Hey, take it easy, Ellis," said Jason. "Don't worry, it won't harm you.

I promise."

Jason took her hand. Even that and his gentle squeezing failed to stop the terrible shakes and the frantic urge to get as far away as possible from this approaching monster, the slowly approaching monster.

"Is that a caterpillar?"

"Look at the size of the thing, Marty," said Lorraine. "Can you imagine the size of the butterfly that it transforms into?"

"Or a moth. Christ, I hate moths."

The shakes had subsided a little but the desire to flee had not left Ellis. Marty was right. It did look like a huge caterpillar. As long as three single decker buses and about as wide. Hundreds of irregular white patches covered its smooth, pale blue skin. Had it sensed them? If it had, the creature showed no indication. It continued along the same path at a consistent speed, about as fast as a walking person. Ellis looked up to Jason, whose gaze was still fixed on the approaching giant. "I'm waiting for you to tell us why you believe that this thing is harmless?"

"The Deltin use these creatures to harvest the food they consume. They're mobile factories. As you can imagine, there's not exactly a lot of vegetation down here. It's not the sort of place where you're going to find a carrot field. It's mainly moss and lichen. Well, that's what these creatures have been built to collect. Oh, and fungi. They collect those too. Once collected, the creatures process the food into all manner of goodies to feed the Deltin population. It's an amazing process, really. No waste either."

"Sounds disgusting."

Jason shrugged. "Yeah, I suppose it does, but it is efficient. The Mantil on the other hand. Well, I think you can guess what those bastards eat." He moved back against the wall and gently pulled Ellis away from the animal. "We'll wait for it to pass, then continue."

"Continue? Where the hell are you taking us, Jason?" Lorraine reached out and glided her fingertips along the huge creature's undulating body. "Oh, that feels weird," she muttered. The woman then turned and glared at Jason. "Fascinating as this may be, and at any other time, I'd be well up for a safari tour around previously unexplored cavern systems, meeting caterpillars the size of trucks which shit out veggie burgers for your insect pals but there are people up above which need our help. You do remember them, Mr. Action Man? You know, human people?"

"Something isn't right with it." Jason pulled Ellis sideways, over to where Lorraine and Marty stood. "We need to move it, guys! Back the way we came." His eyes darted to the left. "Come on, hurry!"

"Wait. You said this was harmless."

"That this is harmless but look at how its middle bit is all jagged. I think something has taken up residence inside! Oh Christ. No wonder this place is deserted!"

He managed to get them close to the archway when Ellis heard what sounded like Velcro being pulled apart. She turned around and saw them. Over a dozen cat-sized insects, covered in dark red shell. They poured out of the jagged hole in the now still caterpillar, scuttled along the width of its body and stopped at the edge. They had to be the scariest looking creature Ellis had encountered so far. Unlike the giants on the surface, these things actually looked intelligent, like they were communicating with each other. What totally freaked her out wasn't just the multiple claws running down their legs or the spider-like over sized teeth. It was what looked like an organic projectile weapon attached to its back. Could these be Mantil warriors?

"Sentinels," hissed Jason. "That must mean the Mantil have infiltrated this section as well. This is bad. Very bad." He crawled closer to the archway. "Follow me, keep quiet and stay down. Don't worry. Those bastard things can't travel through the archways."

Jason pushed her towards the archway.

"You first, Ellis. We'll meet you on the other side."

"I think they know we're here," said Lorraine.

"Right, Marty. Get ready to fire. Aim for their eyes. Lorraine follow Ellis. We'll cover."

Ellis crawled as fast as she could towards the archway. She jumped once and then again when the gunfire started. It was so loud! She felt something brush across her ankle and yelped.

"It's okay, sweetheart," assured Lorraine. "It's only me."

The older woman said something else but another burst of automatic gunfire drowned out her words. Ellis rushed forward and immediately shut her eyes the moment she passed the threshold. She then cried out in shock and pain when she hit solid wall. Ellis knelt back and slammed her palms against the immoveable surface.

"What's wrong with it?"

"How am I supposed to know that?" Ellis stood up. More of those monsters were pouring out of that hole in the caterpillar's body. There's no way Marty and Jason would be able to stop that lot! "Come on, Lorraine." She pulled the pistol out of her waistband and fired into that swarming crowd. She remembered Jason's advice about aiming for the eyes and laughed hysterically. Like that was even possible? All Ellis saw was a mass of teeth, claws, and body. Ellis fired again and again, moaning and weeping, fully aware that their efforts weren't even slowing them down, let alone stopping the tide.

Jason turned around. He looked shocked to see Ellis and Lorraine standing behind them. He pulled Marty up, fired another burst into that fast approaching mass of death then ran over to the archway. Ellis and the older woman kept pace with the men.

She did not want to die, certainly not like this! Ellis looked over her shoulder, expecting her boyfriend to have it figured out, hell, why not? Jason appeared to have an answer for everything at the moment! He looked as confused as Ellis did. She watched him lose his temper over the infernal machinery, hitting and booting the side while knowing that at any second, her life would be coming to an end.

Marty ran over to the archway. Only he didn't join in with the abuse. He simply stopped in front of the device, turned to face Ellis and walked backwards. The man disappeared. Lorraine looked at Ellis. They grabbed each other then ran for the archway. Jason pulled the pistol out of Lorraine's hand. He dropped the assault rifle, spun Lorraine around and pushed her backwards.

"Move it, Ellis. You next!"

The monsters were almost on top of them. "What about you?"

He emptied the magazine into the mass before pushing her inside.

"I'll be right..."

She saw nothing but darkness, then blue light, followed by a grey haze before her feet once again found purchase. Ellis stumbled over Lorraine's body and landed next to Marty. She jumped to her feet and ran back to the archway.

"Where is he?" She grew more anxious by the second and began to fear the worst.

"Any second now, honey," said Lorraine. "I promise."

Ellis bit back the acid retort and tried in vain to prepare herself to acknowledge the simple fact that her Jason was gone for good.

"Maybe there's a time delay, or something? I don't know, or what if the archway took him somewhere else?" Marty glared at Lorraine. "Don't look at me like that. It is possible. I mean, none of us know how this stuff works."

She sank to the floor and rested her back against the door. What was she going to do now?

"Ellis. Come on, girl." Lorraine wrapped her arm around her shoulders. "Marty might be right, you know. Don't give up hope, not just yet."

"Something is happening!" Marty scrambled to his feet and ran over to the girls. "I can feel a rumble. The archway is re-activating."

"It's Jason!"

"What if it isn't?" he replied. "Yeah, I know he said they couldn't come through but what if he's wrong? I mean, something must have used the archway to come through. How else can you explain the soldier confetti?"

Lorraine nodded and helped to pull Ellis onto her feet. She pulled the girl over to the other door. Marty had already reached it and held it open.

"Hurry up!" he cried.

The rumbling increased and an unpleasant smell drifted out from the doorway. It reminded Ellis of bad meat crossed with dirty motor oil. Her heart sank into the pit of her stomach when the truth finally hit home. Marty was right. Her Jason was dead and the massed horde of ravenous insects were trying to come through that archway! Ellis picked up her pace, just as a large black lumpy bag was thrown out of the doorway. It landed on the floor beside one of the tables.

The smell immediately vanished and so did the rumbling. All was still again, except for the mass of slimy black matter, wriggling about on the floor. Ellis looked both at Marty and Lorraine, as if somehow, they knew what had just happened. Lorraine looked at the pistol still in her hand, the only weapon they had left. She handed it to Ellis.

The younger woman took it and tentatively approached this revolting lump. It had stopped moving now and just lay there inert. Ellis took aim.

"Do it!" shouted Marty. "Kill the monster before it kills us."

Ellis still had a knife tucked into her belt. She took it out, dropped to her knees and pressed the tip against the shiny black surface. The voices coming from behind her, urging Ellis to kill it, faded into background noise while she pushed the blade through the film and pulled the knife towards her. The substance split apart like cellophane to reveal a very familiar shape. Ellis dropped the knife and dug her hands inside. Black, foul smelling slop covered everything, making it almost impossible to grab what she most desired.

It took a few attempts but Ellis did wrap her fingers around something solid. She pulled as hard as she could and brought up a wrist, covered in the thick black goo. Once part of the anatomy was free of the stuff 's insidious suction, the rest of the body came up with ease. "Jason!" she cried. "I thought I had lost you forever."

As soon as the relieved words left her mouth, the other two ran over and helped Ellis to pull Jason out of the womb-like bag and to wipe off as much of the vile stuff as they could. Lorraine ripped the arm off her blouse and passed it to Ellis who used the material to clean Jason's face.

The young man blinked a dozen times then lurched forward and threw up.

He shook his head then pulled the cloth out of his girlfriend's hand, found a clean area and wiped his mouth. Their eyes met. "Thank you, Ellis. I thought my time had come just then."

"What happened to you?" asked Lorraine. "What is this stuff?"

He shrugged. "You got me there. Some kind of immobilising agent, I guess. The Sentinels sprayed me just as I was about to dive through the archway."

He tried to stand up. Both Marty and Ellis caught him when his legs collapsed. They sat him in one of the chairs.

"I come bearing gifts by the way. Well, a gift," he said. Jason reached into his jacket pocket, pulled out a small yellow cube and placed it on the table. "I'm sorry to break this to you chaps but, we need to go back through." He held up his hand. "No, don't fret, we aren't going back to that blasted cavern. That's what the cube is for. It'll take us somewhere else. Hopefully, to someone who'll be able to help us sort this mess." He leaned forward. "The situation is even worse than I first believed. What we have here in our lovely town is a beachhead. The Mantil scouts have basically secured a foothold in what they think is enemy territory. If we don't stop them here, their main forces will pour through and that, I'm afraid, really will be the end of everything. Imagine vast armies of genetically augmented, unstoppable, armour-plated killing machines rampaging through every town and city in the country. It won't stop there either, as I guess the other countries will start to panic and they'll do everything in their power to stop those monsters from reaching their shores." He shuddered. "They'll turn this country into a radioactive dust bowl."

Ellis went white. "You mean there's more of those huge monsters down there?"

Jason shook his head. "No, the things already up there are natural. They are the inhabitants from the inner Earth. The things I mean are worse, much worse." He stood up and grabbed the side of the table. Jason quickly shook his head when Marty came to his assistance. "No, I'm fine, it's fine. I'm just a bit weak. Nothing to worry about. I'll be as right as rain in a minute or two." He picked up the cube and slowly walked back to the doorway.

Ellis now noticed a small, rectangular recess in the door frame. Jason pushed the cube into it, turned his head and gave her a wink. The motion looked so painful. Ellis so wanted to hold him but believed that Jason had to feel like he didn't need any help. "Where do you think it will take us, Jason?"

"Let's find out!" He pushed the cube into the recess, took her hand, then stepped through.

Ellis opened her eyes and stared in disbelief at their new environment. She moved a couple of steps away from the archway when Lorraine and Marty stepped into the pale light. As soon as Marty was safely out of the way, the archway merged into the wall. "This has got to be somebody's idea of a joke." Ellis sighed heavily. "Not that I'm finding this remotely funny." She took the lead and walked out of the ladies' toilet and back into the closed market.

CHAPTER ELEVEN
OLD FRIENDS AND NEW ENEMIES

She wasn't sure what was worse; finding herself back in familiar surroundings or, as Jason suggested, walking into yet another unknown environment. Here, in this deserted market, Ellis so wanted to pinch herself, just to make sure that she wasn't actually sleep-walking through some nightmarish part of her brain. Old recollections of happier times and the occasional sad moment jumped, unwanted, into her memory with every step she took. Ellis wished the market still existed, that this place, with its drying bloodstains, its broken stalls and obvious evidence of brutal slaying really did belong inside her warped imagination. Ellis knew, deep down, that the place she remembered with such fondness had gone forever, it would never be the same. Hell, how could it be? Most of the people who either worked in the market or shopped here were fucking dead, munched up fodder for all those vile monsters that invaded this place not so long ago.

"How are you holding up, Ellis?" asked Jason.

"Oh, you know. As well as can be expected, I suppose."

"Are you sure about that?" he quickly glanced to their right.

Lorraine and Marty were inside a shop which sold DIY tools, amongst plastic plates, cheap food, DVD's as well as a million other bits of tat. Lorraine wanted to look for a kitchen knife, at least that's what she said. Right now, she was hitting Marty on the back of the head with an inflatable flamingo.

Jason wiped a couple of tears from her cheek. "Ellis, I know that you're really pissed at me right now and believe me, I do understand why. If I was in your shoes, I would have gone absolutely ballistic. I just hope you can see why I couldn't tell you what I really did for a living?" He tried to crack a smile. "Heck, maybe I should have risked a court marshal and spilled the beans, who would have believed such a fantastic story?　What about if I told you that I was a male stripper, Ellis? That I have a full wardrobe of fake fireman outfits, all with Velcro down each side for easy access? What about a porn star or..."

"Shut up, Jason. Seriously, just stop fucking talking." She shook off his hand, vaguely aware that some of that black stuff now adhered to her fingers too. He spent a good ten minutes earlier on, trying to get the stuff off his skin. Five packets of baby wipes later plus a complete change of clothing, he looked almost normal again, although some of that horrible shit still stubbornly clung to Jason's skin. Ellis walked past the DIY shop and stopped outside a noodle bar. She wrapped her arms around her body while glancing at the menu, while trying to remember the last time she ate. Hell, after the horrors she had been through since this ordeal began, Ellis wasn't sure if she'd ever get her appetite back. Jason had stayed in the same spot, looking like some big dopey puppy. Was he expecting her to run back to him, like the big old cuddly bear act was going to melt her? Ellis kept looking at the menu, while listening to those two in the shop next door comparing previous boyfriend statistics.

How could she even think of eating anyway? She took a deep ragged breath, already knowing the answer. Eating market food is what she did every day. It would prove to her that, despite the hellish circumstances, she could still carry on as if nothing was really happening, giving the middle finger to everything which wanted to do the same to her, to turn poor Ellis into a kebab.

Marty left Lorraine inside the shop and was walking straight for her. "Honey, I'm wondering if you could do me a little favour?!"

Ellis shrugged. "If you want to know Jason's statistics, forget it."

The older man gave her the widest grin she had ever seen. "Very droll. No, just hold both his hands for me, that's all."

She hadn't expected that one.

"It's so he doesn't punch me," he continued. "Your hunky man boy is holding back on something and we need to know what."

A single glance into the shop to find Lorraine looking incredibly uneasy suggested to Ellis that perhaps, looking for a knife might have been an excuse so those two could have a little chin-wag. She had no problem in helping Marty extract a few more info nuggets from Jason. Hell, he might even spout out something that actually made sense! Ellis left the last menu board unread and hurried back to Jason. She grabbed both hands before he had time to react. Her boyfriend sure did react when Marty and Lorraine crowded him from both sides.

"What's the deal, guys? You know, personal space and all that?"

"Shut the fuck up," growled Marty. "You almost got yourself killed going back for that cube, which, as a result, almost caused Ellis to have a mental overload. How about you telling us why you felt it so important to torture the girl?"

Jason's happy-go-lucky persona vanished. Ellis felt the hairs on the back of her neck stand up straight at the sight of the hard-faced killer which took over. It so helped to reinforce her inner argument that Ellis had no idea who this guy really was. Thankfully, the hateful expression dissolved when his eyes made contact with hers. She guessed that her boyfriend wasn't too keen on getting jumped on.

"There were procedures put in place," he said. Jason spoke in hushed tones but it didn't matter, they all heard every word. "The commanders feared something like this might happen, despite the assurances from our new allies. That's why, as soon as the tremors started, the local authorities were secretly put under military control and our own forces, which includes me, I guess, were ordered out into the wilderness." He took a deep breath. "When I say they feared something like this might happen, I meant they thought that some of the wild animals might get free. Don't look at me like that, Lorraine. Believe me, they really did have steps in place to contain any kind of breakout, to put down anything which did get onto the surface without any locals getting hurt. Yeah, so that didn't work so well. Like I said earlier. Our allies held back info, in particular just how close their ancient enemy really was. I suppose, if the top brass knew about the Deltin deception, they might have been more prepared."

"More prepared," sneered Marty. "Listen to yourself, man. You make it sound like your inept fools just took a trip to the shops and forgot to lock the door. What has any of this got to do with you trying to get yourself killed?"

"I was getting to that," he replied. "While our new allies tried to dazzle us primitive cavemen with their magical toys, our own scientists were able to snag one of their little gizmos without our insect pals noticing."

"The cube?"

Jason nodded. "Yeah, the cube. The Deltins had already explained their purpose, that they are some kind of navigation tool. Well, our men in white coats actually figured out how to program them."

Ellis became aware of another noise coming from the other end of the market. It was faint and hard to make out but her neck hairs really started to dance as it sounded like clicking. She looked at Jason who was doing his best to explain to his unreceptive audience that this cube had locked-in coordinates, programmed to take the next traveller to where the top brass would have fled in the event of a full-blown invasion. She pulled her hands away and stepped back. The clicking noise was getting louder. Yet the other three seemed blissfully unaware thanks to their bickering.

"No, Marty, stop asking me that. I don't have a fucking clue as to why it brought us here. I mean, it's not like I set the coordinates is it?"

Her hand brushed across a pile of thick rubber dog balls in a white basket while backing away. Ellis picked up a green one and threw it as hard as she could. It smacked Jason right in the centre of his forehead.

"Hush your lips!" she hissed. "What, are you three deaf or something? We're not alone anymore."

"Nice shot there," he muttered, rubbing his forehead. The man then nodded. "God, I must be losing my edge. Good call, Ellis." Jason pulled several rubber balls out of the basket and handed them out.

"Have you gone insane?" Ellis looked at the two bright red balls that he'd just pushed into her palms then looked down the middle aisle, sure that something down there had just moved.

He shook his head, then grabbed two for himself then ran past the discount shop and the noodle bar. Jason took up position behind a kiddie ride, gestured the others to follow him, then crouched down. Once they were behind him, he pointed to the second-hand shop in the far corner, then threw one of the balls. It smacked into the window, bounced off and rolled across the tiles before coming to a stop next to an ancient red metal weighing machine.

"What are y..."

Jason put his hand over Lorraine's mouth. He then threw another ball. This one flew straight through the open door and vanished inside the shop. A moment later, something large, black and fast smashed into the shop window. The sound of breaking glass seemed to trigger a cacophony of noise.

Ellis wrapped her arms over her head while trying to fight the urge to run away. The clicking had grown to insufferable levels and competed with the loud buzzing of insect wings the length of surfboards. Jason gently lifted her head and she now saw four black beetles standing in a line in front of the shop. The wings belonged to some kind of giant hornet. They hung upside down on the pipes bolted to the ceiling. A moment later, every beetle turned as one then scuttled into the shop. The hornets dropped to the floor and followed them inside.

Jason jumped up. He tapped Lorraine and Marty then raced down one of the aisles. Ellis and the others ran after him.

"Where's he gone?" Ellis skidded to a sudden halt opposite a phone repair stall. Jason was nowhere to be seen.

Marty then pointed to a coffee shop. "He went inside there. I'm sure of it." He pushed past Ellis and hurried forward.

"What's wrong?"

Ellis shrugged. She looked at the rubber balls that Jason had given her. Lorraine had dropped hers by the kiddie ride. Marty had almost reached the coffee shop. Ellis threw one of the balls as hard as she could. It flew over Marty's head and into the shop where it landed on the counter, bounced off and rolled under one of the tables. The interior exploded with a flurry of wings, shell, and legs, as several smaller beasts jumped out from a dozen hiding places. At first, they all fought each other in order to get the ball before two of them suddenly retreated from the scrum. They turned their bright-green mantis-like heads. Marty froze! Ellis threw the remaining ball into the coffee shop which caused all the creatures to resume their scrapping. She ran at Marty, grabbed his arm and pulled him to the side. Lorraine had already taken refuge inside a book stall. Ellis pulled the older man inside.

"Oh my God!" uttered Marty. "They almost got me. I'm sorry, but I don't think I can take much more of this."

Ellis wrapped her arms around his shaking body and hugged him tight. "The word of the day, Marty, is almost. Come on. Get your shit together. Don't lose it now, for God's sake!" She lifted her head. "Lorraine. Where the hell is Jason? Can you see him?"

"Shit. Can you believe we ran straight past him?"

Marty ran over to where Lorraine was leaning. She saw Jason straight away. He stood behind a cold meat counter on the opposite side. The café full of monsters was between them and her boyfriend.

Those things weren't staying inside either. The bastards had already started to scuttle across the flagstones.

"What are we going to do now?" cried Marty. "Throw books at them?"

Ellis ignored the man. She ran to the other side of the stall and leaned over a collection of horror paperbacks. The sit in takeaway belonging to Aroon's dad was in sight and, from what she could see, the route looked clear. Ellis was pretty sure that there were more of those things hiding inside the stalls but as long as they stayed in the middle and stayed quiet, they should be okay. She made her way along the stall and explained her plan to Lorraine. Ellis didn't bother saying anything to Marty. Despite her telling him to stay together, the older man had taken to hugging his legs while rocking from side to side. "Lorraine. Can you sort out Marty?" She reached the counter and silently moaned at just how far the monsters had now spread. The bastards had almost reached the bottom of the book stall. Ellis leaned over the counter and yelped when one of the things reared its head up. She snatched a hardback graphic novel from the clear plastic shelf beside her and hit the damn thing as hard as she could. "Jason!" she shouted. "Meet us at the café!" Ellis had no idea whether he heard as her voice acted as a trigger. Every insect that had left the coffee shop suddenly turned and raced toward the book stall. "Oh fuck!"

Ellis spun around and ran out of the book shop, thankful that Lorraine had managed to get Marty on his feet. They were already at the café and Jason was sprinting along the edge of the shops heading towards them.

"Oh, God, Ellis. You have to run faster!" screamed Lorraine.

She risked a look over her shoulder and saw why. Those insects were right on her tail and gaining on her! "Get inside!"

"We can't, the door's fucking locked and bolted!"

Oh Christ! There was no magic archway to save them this time. They really were screwed.

"I can see a shadow behind the door!" Lorraine pushed past Jason. "Come on," she yelled, while banging on the glass. "I know there's somebody in there. Let us in" Lorraine looked over her shoulder. "Oh God, please!"

A key rattled in the lock. Jason grabbed the handle, pushed it down and slammed the door forward before pulling everybody into the dark shop. Ellis was last to enter. She caught her breath when something hard and sharp touched her back. Lorraine's eyes bulged. The older woman grabbed the front of her blouse and pulled Ellis forward. Jason slammed the door shut.

"Help me out here!" he yelled.

Both Ellis and Lorraine threw their bodies against the door but even with their combined weight, whatever was outside was still managing to open the door! Ellis didn't want to know what Lorraine had seen out there. "Marty, don't just stand there, help us out here!" she cried. The older man didn't even turn his head, he looked comatose. The person who unlocked the door came to their aid instead. "Aroon, thank you, man. You saved our lives."

"Not yet he hasn't," muttered Jason, still trying to turn the key.

Ellis heard the glass behind her back cracking but she dared not move away, knowing that could doom them all. Instead, she did her best to tune out the noise, still her rampant imagination which now had decided to show her a dozen insectile hollow barbs, each one full of glass-eating acid, all scratching the small window and getting reading to punch through the glass and then into her spine. "Shut the fuck up," she hissed. Finally, Ellis heard the sound of the key turning.

"Done it! Jason pulled her away from the door. "Come on," he urged. "All of you. Over to the back wall. It might make them go and hunt somewhere else."

Ellis sat in her usual spot and watched Jason and Aroon barricade the door with a couple of tables. It seemed like a pointless exercise, especially considering her boyfriend had just made it clear that the monsters were not going anywhere if they knew this place was literally packed with tasty human treats. It also occurred to Ellis that this was the first time that Aroon and Jason had met. Granted, it's not like Aroon was her ex-boyfriend or anything except maybe in his mind but Ellis believed that Aroon was the closest friend she really had. It did seem stupid to start thinking about pointless rubbish like that considering their present dire situation but try as she might, Ellis just could not stop that rebellious mind of hers from imagining Jason dropping that table, pulling the other guy across it and stabbing him repeatedly in the chest while accusing the dying man of sleeping with his girlfriend.

Lorraine sat opposite. "Christ. I forgot this place still existed. My mum used to bring me here back when I was a nipper. Back then, an English couple rented it. Their pie and peas were to die for." She looked over at Marty who still hadn't moved, before she turned her attention to Aroon and Jason. They had finished blocking the door and were conversing in low tones next to the till on the counter. "I wish I knew what to do with Marty."

"Let's see what those two are twittering on about before we figure out how to deal with our boy in a coma."

"There's good news and bad news, ladies." Jason sat down beside Ellis and wrapped his fingers around hers. "What do you want first?"

"The bad news, I suppose," answered Lorraine. "Although I can't see how our situation can get any worse, short of those insects finding a way inside."

Jason suddenly looked very tired. His hand squeezed hers.

"I could handle that," he replied. "There's enough sharp knives over there by the counter to turn those things into chopped steak. The problem is, that from what my new pal has just told me, the insects are in no hurry to leave the market. It appears that it isn't as empty as we first believed."

Aroon sat opposite Jason. "We're not the only ones trapped inside," he explained. "Most of the stall owners went to ground when those monsters appeared from nowhere. Some of the customers did too."

"Why?" asked Lorraine. "I mean, I get why you felt the need to hide." She shivered. "Believe me, I really do get that, but what about your homes and your families?"

"Have you seen it outside?" replied Aroon. "You think it's bad in here, well, let me tell you, being inside the market is a walk in the park compared to what it's like out there."

Ellis didn't bother telling the lad that they crossed the outside to get into the market, via a trip to the centre of the fucking planet, obviously. Somehow, she didn't think that tales of humanoid insects, secret agents and teleporters would contribute anything helpful to the conversation. Aroon looked close to breaking point and Ellis had no desire to tip him over. Looking after Marty was bad enough.

"Yeah, we saw how bad it was out there," whispered Lorraine. "Sorry, I have this problem of spurting out words without thinking them through beforehand."

"That's okay." The young man smiled at the woman. He then glanced at Ellis. "I too am afflicted with the same problem." Aroon shuffled in his seat. "That is not to say that people didn't try to get out of here. My father and I saw a few groups attempt to leave. Some were even armed, you know, with shotguns and pistols!"

"You're shitting me!" Lorraine shook her head. "Christ this place really does sell everything."

"Is that a joke?"

"I think it was, Aroon," replied Jason. He turned to Lorraine. "A couple of the larger shops further down are owned by, let me say, 'individuals of questionable morals'. I think it's fair to say that the weapons belonged to those people."

"Are you police or something?" Aroon looked at Jason for a few moments before turning to Ellis. "Is your fella a copper?"

"Something like that. He's kept us alive so far so don't knock it."

"There'll be no knocking from me, Ellis."

"Glad to hear it. I'm guessing they didn't get very far, even with the shotguns?"

He slowly shook his head. "We watched them climb over the back wall. There were four men and two women. Of course we knew them." He glanced at Jason. "We also knew about their reputation. The market isn't that large, and word spreads, you know? Anyway, despite knowing they were bad men, my father and I were still hoping they'd escape and come back with help. Through the gates, we watched them creep along the street, they stayed in the middle of the road, away from the walls. We actually thought they were going to make it. There were a couple of the larger insects visible. Huge brown beetles in the distance and some smaller creatures which kinda resembled ants, but none of them were paying any attention to the people." He took a deep breath. "That all changed when one of the men suddenly made a run for it. The abrupt movement caught the attention of the ants. They rushed towards that running man." Aroon paused. "Sorry."

"It's okay, Aroon. I think we can work out what happened next." Ellis stood up. She hurried over to the counter, grabbed a bottle of juice and brought it back to the table. She placed it in front of Aroon. "Here, this might help."

Aroon unscrewed the top, took a deep swig then replaced the cap. He looked at Lorraine, then returned his attention to Ellis. "I have no idea of the horrors that you four must have experienced since this nightmare began so perhaps you can work out what happened next. Then again, maybe you can't? The ants easily caught up with the running man. Those things really can move. It took them seconds to separate his body into smaller pieces."

"Bloody hell."

"Those three monsters snipped off his legs and his arms then scurried back a couple of metres while this shrieking man lay in the middle of the road while his life fluid pissed out of the four gaping, ragged holes. The bastards didn't do anything else until that poor man's noise finally stopped. Only then did they finish the job and take his head and slice his torso into three smaller pieces." Aroon, took the cap of the bottle, placed it on the table and peered inside the bottle. "You know, my DVD collection is packed with horror movies. Both my parents think it's not healthy to watch movies that, in their opinion, worship and celebrate death. They keep banging on that I should expand my horizons and start watching movies which celebrate life instead." He lifted the bottle and finished off the drink. "I believe that, if I get through this, I shall burn all my DVDs in the back garden."

"Jason, when are the authorities going to arrive? They can't just forget about us."

He held up his hand. "Lorraine, one thing at a time. Aroon hasn't quite finished yet. Please, carry on. What happened to the men with guns?"

"I guess that because they had the shotguns, they'd have no problem in putting down those ants. After all, unlike the beetles, those monsters weren't covered in shell. Plus, there were only three of them. The man in front, the one who tried to stop the other one from running off, walked to the end of the street. He raised his weapon and waited. By this time the ants had eaten that other man. All that remained was a large lake of blood. I guess they must have seen this other long man as yet another meal. They raised their heads and ran, but they stopped suddenly, right at the edge of the road. It didn't matter to the man with the shotgun, their movement had obviously spooked him. He fired twice. One of the ants took both hits but it didn't put it down. Can you believe it?"

Ellis could. They certainly weren't dumb.

"That's when all hell really did break loose. No, that's not right. I mean, it looked like every hellish monster from the depths of hell suddenly appeared. I suppose the sound of the gun must have brought them out of hiding. They came from everywhere. Under cars, out of the trade bins, through the windows, out from behind walls. I've never seen anything like it. I'll be honest, I never saw what happened to the people in the street. Within seconds, the place was full of them, of every type, size and shape. I don't remember seeing any of the really big ones though. Apart from those beetles who stayed where they were. I don't even think those people had time to even scream before that living carpet consumed them."

"And that's what you mean, Jason. About us being trapped in here?" Lorraine sighed. She stood up, walked over to the counter and helped herself to one of the drinks. "So what the hell are we supposed to do now?"

'You said there was good news?" announced a voice from the other side of the shop.

"Marty?" Ellis jumped up and ran over to the man. "Thank Christ you're alright. I thought something had seriously gone wrong with you."

"I think I'm okay," he replied. "I guess the shock must have caught up with me." Ellis helped him to his feet. "I can't believe how hungry I am."

Aroon brought him over a plate of samosas. He handed two to Marty then invited the others to help empty the plate.

Jason took one of the samosas. He then took the plate from Aroon, took it back to the counter and returned with a large chef's knife. "I lied. There is no good news. Only more bad news, I'm afraid. Aroon. I think you had better repeat what you said to me earlier on."

"I think it's better if I showed you." He too went over to the counter and picked up a large knife. He looked over his shoulder. "Follow me please." Aroon then vanished into the next room.

Ellis followed him inside. She'd only ever been back here once, and that was last year when Aroon had asked her to help him bring some cans in to stock up the fridge. She had agreed, partly for curiosity. She had, of course, told him that if he tried anything on with her, she'd throat punch him.

It had shocked Ellis at first to discover just how homely the place looked. Aroon had pointed to the single seat sofa, positioned opposite a huge flat screen TV. He had explained that's where his old man spent most of his time while he had to do all the work. Aroon had told Ellis that while he served customers, cooked the food and cleaned up, his dad sat right there, watching pirated Pakistani action movies while drinking mango lassi.

The contrast to how she remembered the place to how it looked now could not be any starker. It looked like a tornado had been through the room. "Bloody hell, Aroon. It looks like you've been burgled. What the hell happened in here?"

Jason urgently tapped her wrist while violently shaking his head. A moment later, it clicked. Aroon said earlier that he'd watched the carnage outside while standing next to his father. Where was he? Watching Aroon circumnavigate the devastated room, idly picking up a table and kicking pieces of a broken vase under the ripped up sofa, Ellis decided that she didn't want to know what happened to Aroon's father. Something told her that this choice had already been taken out of her hands.

Aroon had reached the far corner of the room by climbing over a table. He stopped beside a wardrobe, turned and coughed. "Sorry about the mess. Weird, really. You know. I mean, even through this, my father still ordered me to clean all the tables, chairs and the counter, while he sat in his chair." He grabbed the sides of the wardrobe and pulled it back a couple of inches. Aroon then walked around the side, pressed his back against the surface and pushed. "Bit harder than I thought." He looked up. "Jason, could you help please?"

Her boyfriend hurried over, shifting the table to the side first. He joined Aroon and helped him push the wardrobe away. Ellis slowly walked towards them, her gaze fixed upon what the wardrobe had previously obscured. Aroon stood beside her.

"My father had no chance at all, really. I mean, we didn't expect them to actually come through the walls. I heard it happen. Well, I heard him shriek out followed by the sounds of struggling."

"Didn't you try to help?"

Aroon glared at Lorraine. "What, you think I cowered under the table and waited for them all to piss off, or something? Of course I tried to help. As soon as I pushed my head through the curtain, my father immediately shook his head, and told me to stay where I was, then when one of them started to turn towards me, my father used the last of his strength to boot it." He looked at them all, one by one. "There were five of six of them in there, with more coming through. What else was I supposed to do?"

Ellis took his hand. "It wasn't your fault, Aroon." She gave his hand a comforting squeeze. "Can you tell me what happened next?"

The lad's gaze shifted to Jason before discreetly pulling his hand out of her grasp. "I'm afraid I went into one of the corners, holding a knife tight while waiting for them to start pouring into the shop. I heard them trashing the back room. It felt like they were in there for hours. None came though, and then the noise abruptly changed to a kind of wet crunching noise. I might have started crying about that time, thinking that those evil fuckers were actually eating my father. I remember standing up and rushing in here, ready to kill them all, and," he sighed, "and I found this."

Marty pushed past them and crouched beside the hole. He gently ran his fingers down the rippled surface. "It feels like glass," he murmured.

"What the hell is it?" Ellis looked at Jason. "Do you know?"

The man just shook his head. "I've not seen anything like this before. It certainly isn't something the Deltin do anyway."

Aroon gave Jason a curious look but kept quiet. Ellis peered over Marty's head trying to make sense of what they were seeing. It was a fabricated tunnel made from, she guessed, a secreted resin. It must run the length of the market, going through the middle of every shop on this side. Aroon climbed inside. "What the hell are you doing?"

"Don't worry. It's strong enough to support our weight," he replied. "This is what I need to show you."

Marty was the first to follow Aroon inside. The man had not stopped touching the damn stuff. Ellis climbed in next. She did everything she could to avoid touching the resin. It felt repulsive, like frozen dead flesh but warm. Aroon moved a little further down the corridor and as she followed, Ellis spotted a junction.

"This is it," Aroon said.

The junction opened out into a clothing shop. Ellis recognised the place almost immediately. She bought a pair of jeans from here a few months ago and had to bring them back because she didn't realise until she got home that there was a rip in the leg. She remembered that old witch of a shopkeeper trying to convince Ellis that it was the fashion and they'd been made like that. It took her ages to get the money back and she would never forget the face the woman pulled after Ellis bid her a good day and walked out of the shop.

She was still here, but encased in some kind of pod-like structure which hung from the ceiling. It wasn't the only pod in here, dozens of them filled the interior. "Oh my God. What's happening to them?"

"My father is in one of these, I think. He might even be in the next chamber, or the one after that. I'm not really sure to be honest."

"Fuck."

Ellis tore her gaze away from the pods. "Jason?"

"I know why the archway brought us back here. It wasn't a mistake at all. I know what's happening now. I think the Mantil are collecting humans and converting them into their own kind. That must be what this is. It's a hatchery and if we don't find some way to stop them, we are going to be in serious trouble!"

CHAPTER TWELVE
TOOLED UP AND READY TO ROCK

A few moments ago, the damn gun became more a hindrance than a help when it got in Andrew's way and he went arse over tit and ended up on the floor. To make matters worse, the fall had reopened his leg wound. The temptation to wang the bloody thing almost got the better of him but instead of throwing what might come in useful later on, he laid it on top of a second-hand washing machine, intending to return for the weapon when he'd retrieved some actual shells for the bloody thing. Andrew now felt as naked as the day he was born, armed with just his damn knife. Granted, it had saved his bacon a couple of times but only against the smaller specimens that he'd run, or limped into.

Andrew needed to go back and check out that locked-up shop. Surely they must have dispersed by now? He hurried along the edge then stopped without knowing why, apart from his neck hairs standing up. Andrew spun around, hoping to Christ that one of those bastards weren't behind him. Thankfully, he found himself still alone. What the hell could that have been? His eyes informed him that there wasn't anything close by, that is, until Andrew just happened to look towards where he'd laid his gun.

"You have got to be shitting me!" he whispered. The shotgun had vanished! Andrew limped back to the shop, thinking that perhaps it might have just kinda fallen off. He wanted to slap himself upside the head. Kinda fallen off? What was he now, a retard or something? Some fucker had stolen the bloody thing. Andrew stopped in front of the washing machine. Besides, if it had fallen off, it would be right there, lying next to that silver dryer.

What pissed him off more than anything was his inability to yell out. Not after the last occasion when he'd opened his gob. Christ on a bike. Andrew shuddered. No, he didn't want to go through that nightmare again.

Andrew just happened to stumble across the shuttered up shop again. The fact that he'd walked full circle hadn't really bothered him. What pissed him off more than anything was the fact that his best buddy, that shitty scumbag, Nelson, had lied to him. Both bolts were off and lying on the floor. The devious bastard must have unlocked them earlier, meaning he fully intended to kill Andrew first before returning here to stock up. At that moment, Andrew might have yelled out a few choice insults. He couldn't remember the exact words, nor did it matter. It was the consequences which counted, namely the appearance of over a dozen of those bastard insects, all craving one thing: Andrew's soft insides.

It took him a good ten minutes to lose them all. Even so, Andrew almost ended up as dinner twice. Thankfully, a shop selling pots and pans saved him. Andrew took refuge in there while fleeing from a particularly persistent pair of bright yellow termite type creatures. They ended up meeting the business end of a copper bottom frying pan.

Whilst inside that shop, it occurred to Andrew that this was as good a time as any to get the fuck out of there, meet up with Tony, if he was still alive, and get the hell out of Dodge. He hurried over to the other door which led out onto the main street and took a look outside. Any hope of escaping evaporated when he saw just how many of those things were out there now. Andrew wouldn't get ten yards past the door without one of those huge monsters charging him, pulling off his head and scoffing the insides. Whether he liked it or not, Andrew had to face the simple fact that he was stuck in here for the foreseeable future.

He took a single step back, placed his hands on his hips and scanned the immediate area. From this vantage point, Andrew saw into four stalls and one shop behind him. He saw nothing out of place, not that he expected to, it wasn't going to be that easy. Andrew had to face the fact that he'd lost the gun. There was no way he was going to start poking his head into the shops, not a chance of that. Andrew preferred to keep his head attached, thank you very much. Hell, if he had felt suicidal, that katana, hung on the wall inside that shop directly in front of him would already be in his hands by now. The insects had to be somewhere, and as they weren't roaming the aisles, the only place left were the market stalls, lurking out of sight, just waiting for their unwitting prey to trip over them, then bam! Insect dinner.

"Sneaky fuckers," he muttered under his breath. Andrew spun around and retraced his steps, intending to get back to that shuttered up shop. He made his way back to the market edge and limped from pillar to pillar, keeping an eye out for any movement coming from those dark interiors. There were sliding shadows and the occasional movement of what could be either leg or claw but nothing raced out to catch him.

He heard the unmistakable sound of something heavy being dragged across the tiled floor. It came from the market interior. Andrew froze as three humanoid shapes appeared from behind a kebab stall. Oh fuck, it was the things from his vision. The insect-men. Christ on a bike, so they did exist after all! Andrew quickly shifted to the left so the concrete pillar obscured his body. He tilted his head and watched them pull something down the aisle. Andrew couldn't tell what it was due to a bright-orange fabric sheet covering the bulk. Whatever was under there was big and heavy, due to how those things were struggling with it.

They pulled it, inch by inch, down the aisle. The insect-men dragged the object past where Andrew hid and finally pushed it against the front of a hardware shop. The cover slipped off the huge object to reveal, what looked to Andrew, to be an arched door. He barely had time to comprehend the significance of this new development before the three figures totally blew his mind by standing in front of this archway, uttering a string of clicking and buzzing sounds before vanishing into thin air.

It took him a moment to work out that the insect-men hadn't exactly vanished, they had somehow walked into that archway. Andrew waited for a few moments before he ran over to where they had once stood. He saw little point in trying to explain to himself what he'd just seen. Where was the point in that? The practical side of him did spot a potential way out of this damn market. As insane as it sounded, Andrew might be able to follow them through to wherever the fuck they went.

He took a hasty step back. No, of all the stupid ideas he'd come up with today, that one really did need to go right to the top of the flagpole. Christ knows what could be waiting for him through there. Andrew might be trapped in here due to the insect army outside generally running down and tearing apart any human foolish to step outside but at least he was still alive.

Andrew jumped back again when he heard a low hum coming from the archway. Did that mean he'd inadvertently activated it? He spun around, or how about some more of those things heading this way and remotely activating the damn thing?

The hum increased in volume! Andrew took one last look at the weird gizmo before running back into the retro arcade, knowing that if more were coming then hiding behind that pillar would not save his arse.

He took up position behind one of the arcade cabinets and waited to see if there really were any more of those things on their way. Andrew had no intention of staying in here for any longer than necessary, not after what happened the last time. The noise coming from that gizmo had changed to a high-pitched warbling sound. It fair hurt his ears. He decided to give it a couple more minutes and if nothing of interest happened, then he really would move out. Andrew still had to make his way back to that other shop to see exactly what lay beyond those metal shutters. In fact, what was there to stop him from taking enough food and drink with him in there? If there really were weapons inside then all he had to do was to close the shutters behind him and hold out until help finally arrived. Andrew nodded to himself. Yeah, that idea was golden, a lot sodding better than wandering around here armed with a crappy knife, that's for sure. Staying out in the open was basically the equivalent of signing his own death warrant.

Andrew slipped out from behind the cabinet and moved further inside the arcade, making sure that he could still see outside. So concerned with watching for activity beyond the arcade entrance, he forgot about any possible hidden obstacles inside. Namely, what remained of his old partner, Nelson. His foot landed right in the middle of where the man's head had landed.

"Oh hell," he muttered, lifting up his leg to reveal a thick coat of grey slime attached to the sole of his shoe. Andrew gazed down at the mess; despite the disgust he felt, it really did shock him at how little of Nelson remained.

"I have a cloth in my back pocket if you want to use it, dude."

Andrew jumped. He turned a little too quickly and almost lost his balance. Only his quick reactions and a conveniently placed change machine stopped him from falling face first into the stinking muck staining the carpet.

"Sorry, dude. Didn't mean to scare you there."

The apparition was back. Standing in his usual spot, leaning, as casual as you like, against that sit-down arcade cabinet and sporting a grin which, thanks to Andrew's current mood, so needed slapping off.

He reached into his back pocket and pulled out a yellow duster that had seen better days. "It'll only cost you one shiny pound coin. Now, I think that's an excellent trade, dude."

"Tell me why you're here."

"Does this mean you're not going to hand over a pound? Man, I thought we were pals. I mean. I did save your life, or have you forgotten about that?"

Andrew lifted his leg and scraped off the mess using the hard edge of the change machine. It had already occurred to him that the appearance of this apparition was no coincidence. This guy obviously knew something about that structure outside. He wasn't going to ask though as Andrew just didn't care. The cloth and the pound coin swap had a deeper significance here and he was pretty sure that Mr. Geek over there had plans for Andrew which no doubt involved him getting his arse bitten off. He'd already made up his mind to hide out inside that shuttered up shop and wait for all this to blow over. It was the sensible thing to do.

He fished out a coin from his pocket and flipped it towards him.

"There you go. A pound coin. Now go do one. I've stuff to take care of."
Turning his back on the apparition was, in Andrew's mind, the most
effective method of terminating this conversation before it started. He
walked towards the entrance, this time avoiding the stain, and took one
last glance at the structure before heading outside, his thoughts already
turning to the best place to acquire adequate supplies without running
into any more of those insect things.

He blinked and found himself back in the arcade, leaning against
that sit-in game. The geek sat beside him, yet again trying to beat that
high score. Andrew so wanted to explode, to reach into that cabinet, pull
him out and punch him into the middle of next week. He suppressed the
urge, partly because he wasn't even sure that would happen but mainly
due to the fact they now had an audience looking down from the balcony.
Tony had joined Nelson who gave Andrew a little wave. Nelson just
glared at him, not that he expected any less.

"The fact that you did toss over some cash is the only reason why I
didn't let you blindly wander into what could well have been your certain
death." He took his eyes off the screen for a second. "Do you really want
to join your pals, Andrew?" He returned to the game. "Granted, Nelson is
deader than dead now. You made sure of that. As for poor Tony? Well,
the insect warriors pulled his kicking and screaming body out of that car
and stuck him in one of those cocoons. The enzymes are converting him
as I speak. Just like they're converting me."

The huge insects were outside the arcade again, which kinda
restricted his choices a little. There would be no running up the stairs this
time either. Andrew was pretty sure that those two goons would give him
a good kicking. Nelson especially. The old bastard wasn't exactly a
looker but he still had the charm to pick up the odd MILF in one of the
many clubs in the city. The shotgun blast to his face buggered that up for
him. Not to mention the flight over the balcony. The fact that he was also
dead probably put a spanner in the works too.

Had he totally lost his fucking mind? Just what the hell was all that
about? The old bastard couldn't hurt him, no more could the monsters out
there. This was all some deranged hallucination, caused by this tosser.
Andrew clenched his fist. All he had to do was drop the cunt and walk
out. Simple as.

"I bet that, right now, you're thinking that none of this is real, that it
can't harm you?" The young man climbed out of the cabinet. "It probably
isn't a good idea to put that theory to the test, dude. Got another pound
coin by the way?"

"What do you want with me?"

"Oh, so you can talk, and you vomit out a direct question." He grinned. "That's a great start, cutting the small talk down to the bone. That's uber cool. I can work with that. What do I want, you cry? Oh, that's an easy one, dude. I want you to kill me before the conversion process is complete. I also want you to follow those warriors back to their staging post and somehow put a spanner in the works."

"Oh, is that it? I thought that, you know, you wanted me to do something really difficult."

"Wait, is that sarcasm?"

Andrew reined back the desire to hurt the kid when his expression lost the pretend street-wise look. Christ, he now looked about twelve.

"I don't want to hurt my mum and dad, man," he whispered. The lad took a deep breath. "Or my mates, or any of my family. That's what will happen, Andrew. When the conversion finally turns us all into those murderous things. The first step is to eliminate every person who you're attached to and..." He clicked his fingers. The representations of Andrew's colleagues vanished and the giant insects faded away. "Why am I even bothering? Forget it. Just leave me alone."

He didn't even bother arguing, Andrew simply turned and found himself back where he should have been. The arcade had now gone dark. None of the machines were playing and all the lights were out. If the kid was trying to guilt-trip Andrew into doing his bidding then the daft twat obviously didn't know him. He sighed heavily. "Christ, what a loser."

That annoying distraction had cost him at least ten minutes. Time that Andrew could have spent picking up essential supplies in readiness for his attempt to sit out the rest of this disaster in relative peace and comfort. Then again, ten minutes, an hour or ten hours, he supposed it didn't matter all that much as long as by the end of it, he was safely stowed away inside that shuttered up shop.

The only shop he found which looked safe enough to enter sold Polish food. Andrew didn't recognise any of the labels. He grabbed a plastic bag and added a couple of jars of what looked like meatballs. Beggars can't be choosers. Andrew added a few packets of biscuits and a couple of water bottles. Before leaving, he threw in a few more meatball jars, just to be sure.

Just as he left the shop, laden with his goodies, Andrew glanced back at the dark arcade, and the insane thought of actually going back inside and doing what the kid begged took root and no matter what he did, the thought wouldn't budge. "Bollocks to that," he whispered. Andrew walked backwards, while watching the arcade entrance. No, he wasn't going back in there, not without lighting. Hell, he had already witnessed the carnage that those things protecting the cocoons could do. It was all very well the kid saying that they wouldn't harm Andrew but that might change if he went back inside with the sole purpose of wrecking another one.

He turned around after he reached the shutters, placed the bag by his feet, crouched down and got ready to lift the shutter.

The smell hit him even before Andrew had the shutters to ankle level. He moaned, partly in disgust but mostly in frustration. He knew exactly what awaited inside the ship and it sure as hell wasn't a handy cache of weapons. Andrew slammed the metal shutter up past his head and looked at the dozens of foul smelling cocoons, hanging in five neat rows going down the length of the shop. He let go of the shutter and stepped back, feeling that his whole world had just come to an end. Until now, Andrew hadn't understood just how important this plan had been to him. It was, in essence, the only thing left to aim for.

Somewhere inside the market, a couple of those insects started up with the clicking. A moment later, a few more joined in. Andrew dropped to his knees then pressed his hands against his ears when it sounded like the whole insect population in here were clicking. They were laughing at him, that's what they were doing. Fucking laughing, having a bit of a humorous clicky banter at his expense. The bastards obviously found it fucking hilarious that he was utterly unable to do anything right. He'd fucked up the bank job, lost both the money and his colleagues and to put a big fat cherry on top of the cake, he'd gone and gotten himself trapped right in the middle of some kind of apocalyptic invasion. So, sure they were laughing.

"You're all going to be laughing on the other side of your deformed faces when I finish with you," he growled. Andrew looked up. The arcade was once again bathed in the bright milky blue glow coming from all those arcade games.

He jumped up and stormed back into the retro arcade. Andrew walked straight down the middle aisle, not even bothering to step over the squelchy carpet, which still contained a lot of the bodily fluid belonging to Nelson. He ran up the metal and didn't stop until he reached the chrysalis.

"Right, so here I am, you manipulating piece of shit. What's it going to be then? A throat punch, if I could find it, or do I throw you over the railing like I did with Nelson?" He received no reply. Andrew looked around where he stood, in search for anything he could use to hack through the chrysalis. He figured that even if he did throw the damn thing over the railing, it's likely that the shell could cushion the impact.

That fungal-like growth now covered every part of the body inside the cocoon. That wasn't the only change since Andrew was last here. The cocoon now had a bulging protrusion which ran from the floor all the way up to the top of the chrysalis. Like the rest of the surface, the skin was semi-transparent, and it didn't take him long to figure out what it could be.

"The geek said this was converting them into warriors." He carefully placed his fingers on the bulge and exerted a little pressure. The material cracked like an egg shell allowing him to reach inside, through the gelatinous fluid surrounding the object and touch it. "A warrior has to have some kind of weapon," he murmured.

Andrew grabbed the shaft and pulled. It gave some resistance but not enough to stop him from freeing the object from its binding. "Come to daddy," he purred. It didn't look like any weapon that he'd ever seen, at least, not in general service but that didn't mean that Andrew hadn't seen something like this in the past, but those things belonged inside the furtive imaginations of all the geeky idiots who developed a boner from watching TV shows about aliens and various other bollocks and nonsense.

He stared at his find, while trying to figure out what to do with it now. Warm slime dripped over the back of his hand. Andrew wiped some of it off and as his other hand brushed over the thin shaft, his fingers must have had some kind of mechanism hidden on the surface as what he assumed to be the business end lit up like a Christmas tree!

The activation sequence wasn't just relegated to a physical sense. Andrew also felt a presence crawling up his spine. At first, he thought the geek was back but that thought quickly vanished. Fuck, no. This wasn't the geek

This mind was stronger, much stronger than the kid's. It also felt alien and cold, so cold! The invading thoughts slimed over his own mind and sank inside, leaving Andrew feeling like it had despoiled him.

"What the fuck just happened to me?"

[Still your precious thoughts, human. I think we are going to be good friends, don't you?]

The voice came from him, from within his own head! Andrew gritted his teeth in both shock, frustration and terror, knowing exactly what had happened to him. The weapon, this damn thing clasped in his hand was no inert piece of machinery. The fucking thing was alive and its mind had joined with his.

A calming sensation spread through his body. That outside invader had done this, the bastard was making him high using Andrew's own pleasure chemicals. Not that he cared, Well, he didn't now anyway.

[Use me, Andrew. Use me for your first time, my lover. Let us cement our bond with your first shot.]

He turned the business end towards the chrysalis, the weird sultry and frankly, well, fucking disturbing voice wasn't the only addition. Andrew now knew exactly how to use this ultra-advanced piece of insect tech.

[Could you raise the Ganthis staff a little higher, lover boy?] purred the voice. [I think it's best if you stand back another pace too. There are a few chemicals inside that shell that are more than a little volatile and won't respond kindly to a blast of concentrated stream of energised plasma. We don't want you to lose any of those pretty fingers do we? I can't explain the pleasure they give me when they caress my body, Andrew, and I'm so looking forward to lots more prolonged contact as we become more familiar.]

He did as she suggested while wondering if there was any way of getting rid of that voice: she was seriously freaking him out.

Andrew fired. The cocoon simply liquefied. He looked at the staff in absolute awe as the warm fluid ran between his feet.

[As much as I want you to stay here, beautiful, with that warm and soft hand resting against my surface, I think you need to finish the promise you made to the previous occupant. The Reslslin guardians have just detected another loss. This close to hatching is making them a little nervous. Andrew, you so need to move. I don't know what I'd do if I lost you.]

He spun around and ran back down the metal steps, fully aware that the ceiling had begun the move. Andrew remembered how quickly those things dealt with the last threat. Even with this remarkable new gun, it's doubtful that he'd last more than a few seconds. He reached the sit-down cabinet wondering if the weapon would even fire on its own kind.

That answer presented itself a second later when four of the guardians dropped onto the top of a pennyfalls machine. Even before they leapt, Andrew knew where the bastards were going to leap next. They would be landing on him! He brought up the staff and fired again. This time, the blast took out the potential attackers as well as most of the glass in the machine.

He raced out of the arcade, listening to the outraged squeal coming from hundreds of guardians. "Oh, shit," he uttered, looking at all the insects gathering by the edge of the arcade. "I really have booted a wasp nest there. Are those things going to come after me?"

[No, sweetheart. None of the remaining Reslslin guardians will hurt a single hair on your sexy body. I cannot voice for the other creatures still inside this place. Their calling is bound to attract their attention. You should leave right now, while you still can.]

Andrew saw shadows in the middle of the market start to move and knew that he really did have no choice but to get out of here while he still could. He reached the archway and stood in front of the structure. "Now what?"

[I'm accessing the control matrix right now, lover boy. Please stand by.]

Just before the archway 's hidden systems hummed into life, Andrew suddenly wondered just how much of what he had just gone through had really happened.

CHAPTER THIRTEEN .

Captain Dallas Penistone's keen sense of hearing picked out the noise of a tin can clattering against stone. Weapons fire coming from both human and insect forces should have totally drowned out the otherwise inconspicuous noise. This didn't stop the man from throwing himself into a pile of old carrier bags. The movement saved his life as a moment later, a blast from one of their infernal weapons melted out an ovoid section from the corner of the stone building that he'd been sheltering behind.

The urge to get the fuck away from there before the clown fired again grabbed hold of him but he choked that bastard down as neat as you like. Running meant instant death, maybe not from the one hiding in the alley who had just tried to turn him into meat soup but certainly from one of its pals who were hiding out in the upper floors of the many commercial premises surrounding him and what remained of his squad.

He dug himself deeper, confident that the noise of battle would mask the rustling coming from the bags and waited, feeling confident that, although he was currently incapacitated, one of the others would remove the menace.

A moment later, a stream of Hi-Ex shells turned the entrance to the alleyway into dust and rubble. Dallas thought he heard a scream but that might have just been wishful thinking.

His guys might not have any of those fancy ray guns but they could still bite those scrawny bugs on the arse when the need arose. He risked lifting his head, keeping his gaze on the windows of those grey, monolithic tower-blocks surrounding his position, alert for any tell-tale signs of movement. Unlike human snipers, the insect guys just couldn't stay still for more than a few seconds. The skittish things continuously gave away their hiding places, making it a piece of piss for his guys to take them out.

Nothing above him moved and as the alleyway was now completely blocked, Dallas judged it safe enough to join his men. He rolled away from the bags, scrambled to his feet and raced back to the relative safety of the transit van on the other side of the street. The remainder of his unit didn't look all that happy to see him return. Dallas didn't blame them, considering it had been his idea to try to reach the interior of that newsagents in the first place.

Captain Yates, the ultimate pain in his arse, couldn't resist smirking. He had suggested going left, picking their way through the line of abandoned cars and head towards the new shopping centre. He believed that's where the others would be holed up. Dallas had asked how he was even sure that any others had survived the initial battle but the smug bastard simply gave him that dazzling smile. The one that had seemed to even win over his own men, at least for a few seconds.

He sat down with his back to the van and gratefully accepted a bottle of warm water given to him by Henderson. "Thanks," he replied, after returning the bottle to the man. Henderson packed the bottle away and grabbed his rifle, as he leant against the side of the van. "Good shooting, by the way."

The soldier grinned. "Barbecued insect. All we need is a little soy sauce, some peppers and a keg of beer and we'd be sorted for the rest of the day."

"Do you ever stop thinking about your stomach, Henderson?"

The last member of their unit blew through his teeth in what sounded like annoyance to Dallas before the young NCO returned to lookout duty.

"Come on, you miserable sod. Don't pretend that you haven't imagined what they taste like. Okay, I'll be the first to admit that raw, their insides do look a bit like a cross between custard and frogspawn but, saying that, liver looks fucking gross until you cook it."

Corporal David Jenkins growled under his breath. "Captain, please can you tell that disgusting slob to shut his hole?"

Henderson just laughed. "Oh yeah? I'm guessing you have already forgotten about Bolivia then. I haven't. That fry up we had after a week of jungle training? You scoffed every bit of that repast. Crunching on those cooked bugs like they were finest nuts."

"We hadn't eaten for two days, you plank. That's completely different. That was survival."

Dallas allowed himself to get lost in amongst their banter. It actually brought a perverted sense of normality to this extraordinary situation. It reminded him of just how much shit they had been through in the past four years. Obviously, in previous incursions, their enemy were human, even so, if you put took out the fact that these buggers were basically six-foot cockroaches with intelligence and a shitty attitude, there really wasn't much to differentiate the insects from a bunch of brain-washed Jihadis armed with AK47s or Central American Drug dealers. Well, apart from the insects carried superior weaponry. That reminded him. "How's our inventory looking, Jenkins?"

"It's in a bit of a sorry state, sir. Even if the enemy sightings stay as light as they currently are, I don't think we're going to last more than a few hours. If they lead another assault, well," Jenkins shrugged. "A few minutes is the best I can offer."

"We would have had a little bit more ammo if you hadn't wasted our last hi-ex on killing the stone wall, soldier."

Dallas could have quite happily shot that man in the face. That bastard had done it again. What was wrong with the man? Banter was all very well, it helped the men gel, to be a more effective fighting unit, but to throw out barbed comments like that did nothing but wind the men up, like they weren't already wound up tighter than a damned clock. Both Henderson and Jenkins didn't rise to the man which helped matters, even so, Dallas would have to have a quiet word with their new Captain at some point, if, that is, they managed to get out of this mess in one piece.

"So, it's obvious, we need to re-supply."

"And I've been saying that from the get go!" snapped Yates. "Sooner rather than later too. Now, if we had gone with my plan, we would be halfway there already." The young Captain climbed over Jenkins and peered around the side of the front of the van. "The route that I suggested is still clear." he looked back at Dallas. "Well?"

"No way," snapped Henderson. "You're not our Commander." He pointed at Dallas. "He is. Besides, we have our orders."

Captain Dallas noticed Jenkins nodding in confirmation, and as much as he wanted to disregard everything that vomited from the jumped-up little tosser's gob, right now, he might actually be correct. The safety of his men was paramount, even if it meant disobeying orders. He sighed. "Lead the way then, Captain."

Christ, could the new addition to their diminished squad look any smugger? When the officer's back was turned, he shook his head at his men, hoping they'd take his signalling as a sign not to make any waves.

"I'm glad you reached the right decision," said Yates. "I'm kinda surprised that you weren't already on your way." He glanced over his shoulder. "I am still not sure why you were heading to the old market, old chap."

Dallas glared at that sunny-side-up smile for a moment before returning to a neutral gaze. "I was simply following orders, Captain. We were to meet up and join Bravo Company. They were escorting survivors through the top part of the town, controlled by the enemy and needed back-up."

"Right. Well, I'm sorry to be the bearer of bad news, Captain but Bravo company no longer exists. As for the survivors?" He shrugged. "We both know their fate."

"Wait on!" cried Jenkins. "How the hell can you possibly know that? We've had no communication for hours now."

Dallas half expected the Captain to give them another smug grin followed by a tap on the side of his nose, which might have really earned the bastard a bullet in his brain. Thankfully, at least for Yates, the man replied with a cryptic answer of having 'other means' of communication. Dallas let that lie, already aware that the Captain was no ordinary soldier. He'd already guessed he was special forces. His whole superior attitude was his biggest clue, that and the fact this joker actually knew who the enemy was.

"Good, now we're all singing from the same hymn book, let's get a move on. We don't have much time. The hatching will be well under way by now, meaning we could end up fighting hundreds more of the damned things." He smiled his annoying smile. "And you thought the wildlife was bad enough? Believe me, that was just target practice compared to what's coming!"

Both Henderson and Jenkins looked at Dallas, obviously wanting answers that he was unable to give. He just shrugged, having no idea what this joker was prattling on about. It did confirm his suspicions that Yates did know far more about this situation than he'd been letting on. Dallas waited until the Captain was clearly out of earshot before calling Jenkins and Henderson over. "We'll follow him for the moment but the second it looks like he's trying to get us killed, we'll hold him down and beat the necessary info out of him. Deal?" He hadn't seen the pair smile so much.

Dallas caught up with the Captain who'd taken shelter behind a Ford Escort. He pointed to a clothes shop on the other side of the road.

"There's two of them hiding in there," he whispered. "We need to take them out but without making any noise." Yates nodded to an electronics store further on. "I think there's three more on the second floor. Any gunfire is bound to alert them to our presence."

Dallas couldn't see any sign. He was about to ask if he was sure when something moved past one of the second floor windows. "Shit," he muttered. Dallas grabbed Henderson. "Stay with the Captain. Keep quiet, keep out of sight and," he glanced at Yates, "and behave yourself. Jenkins, you're with me."

He doubled back, ran low along two cars, then raced over the road. Dallas popped his head over the boot of a grey Honda, saw nothing moving then gestured Jenkins to catch up. He crawled around the side of the car then threw himself into the alcove of a junk shop. According to Yates, their targets should be in the next shop. They were bound to be alert so they couldn't just walk in next door and hope the insects didn't notice them. Another method was needed. He tried the door. It was unlocked. Dallas silently entered the dark shop, waited for Jenkins to enter before he shut the door after him.

"You ready to skewer some tasty insect for Henderson's barbecue?"

"I'd rather stick that Captain. There's something about him that proper makes my skin crawl." Jenkins silently moved through the shop and reached the window close to the counter. He pulled the blind down a crack. "Sorry, that was uncalled for. He is an officer, I suppose."

Dallas joined him at the window. He saw the two men crouched behind the car as well as a couple of giant bugs in the distance. They weren't doing anything that could be perceived as a threat. It surprised him to find any of the really big ones left alive.

It was those bugs which really ate up their supplies of ammunition, not the things that came after. Perhaps that snotty Captain out there had forgotten that bit. Perhaps, if that bastard had told them there and then that the giant bugs weren't the real problem then maybe his squad wouldn't be in this dire situation. Maybe his squad would still be complete. Dallas turned his attention back to the two soldiers for a moment before moving away from the window.

What else was that Captain hiding from them? Feeding him piecemeal if and when the snotty Captain felt like it was not classed as a transparent relationship. Dallas had his men, what was left of them, to look after, to stop them becoming dead, whereas he suspected Yates only cared about himself. In fact, Dallas was sure of this fact. That bastard would probably throw them all under the wheels of a bus if it meant saving his hide. This unhealthy line of thinking only ended with the one outcome. To remove the one factor in their unit which didn't fit. To whack Yates before he did the same to them.

"Sir, are you okay? You've gone a strange shade of cream."

"I'm fine," he replied. Dallas was far from fine. What the hell was wrong with him? The enemy was out there, the bad guys were quite recognisable this time. Dallas had sworn an oath to protect his country as well as honour the uniform and what he'd been contemplating would only lead to him getting shot as a traitor.

Did the obligation to protect his men outweigh the potential ramifications of hurting a fellow officer? After all, Dallas had no doubt that if Yates hadn't appeared on the scene, his unit would still be intact. Davis and Lovejoy wouldn't have ended up as beetle food.

Yates must have known the evolved insect soldiers would arrive yet this didn't stop him from warning his men to conserve their ammo. There they were killing those things like it was a turkey shoot at a carnival, believing that once the monsters were dead, they'd all receive medals and praise before heading home for a nice cup of tea. Those giant insects never stood a chance, not against their superior fire-power. Those hard insect shells might have deflected light rounds but armour-piercing bullets simply shredded their insides. Even the flyers, as frightening as they were, ended up spiralling out of the sky with the help of their trusty assault rifles. Hell, his men didn't even need to finish off the wounded. Their own did that for them.

All the while, that smug fucker who appeared out of nowhere, stood there, with that familiar shit-eating grin plastered on his mug, complimenting his men on their expert shooting. Laughing and joking with them as his unit turned this town into a vast killing ground.

Where was he when Lovejoy was taken by that beetle? The poor bastard had just walked past a record shop when those black legs, covered in serrated barbs snapped out from inside that smashed shop-front and pulled the shrieking boy into the darkness. Yates had stood there, like some useless clown while shouting out that he was dry. Lovejoy had flown past the captain and straight into the shop, closely followed by Dallas and his remaining unit. They had found what remained of Lovejoy and Davis at the back of the shop. There hadn't been enough human parts left to pack into a travel suitcase.

They had spotted the murderer of their two men right at the back of the shop, huddled into a corner. Henderson shone a torch on it. The damn thing didn't even twitch, too busy pushing small lumps of bloodied meat into its mouth. Henderson had taken care of that vile creature with a burst of gunfire.

Dallas tapped Jenkins on the shoulder. "Come on, soldier. Let's get this done and dusted."

The man nodded. He stood up and followed the Captain as they slowly made their way through the junk shop. Dallas stopped beside an open door. It just occurred to him that during the slaughterfest, that other captain hadn't fired a single shot. Did that mean the man was dry before he even met up with his unit or had he been lying? If the latter, then he was responsible for the deaths of two of his men come to think of it, even if Yates was dry, the coward still allowed them to die. Hell, Lovejoy must have been out as well but that didn't stop him from trying to rescue his mate.

"Question for you, Jenkins. Can you recall anyone, apart from Henderson, discharging their weapons whilst inside that record shop?"

The soldier shook his head. "No, sir. I can't. Why, is it important?"

"No. I'm just wondering about noise. About how much it would matter to our current situation if we just put a bullet into those insectoid heads instead of stabbing the bastards." Dallas had no idea why he just lied. "Don't worry about it, Jenkins. It's probably best to stick to the plan and save our ammo." If he shared his doubt with either Jenkins or Henderson, the Captain would have wished that beetle had got him. "You know, I bet that somewhere in here there could be a whole host of weaponry we could utilise. Crossbows and axes spring to mind. Maybe even a katana." Dallas knew that they had no time to start rummaging through all this junk in the hope they might stumble over another weapon but he thought best to voice the notion simply to take the other man's mind away from killing Yates.

"Don't worry about me," said Jenkins, pulling an eight inch matt-black combat knife out from a leather sheaf. "This darling is eager to bite into the flesh of our enemy." He slowly smiled. "Whether it's insect or human. It'll make no difference to her."

Hell, so much for taking his mind away from killing the other Captain. Jenkins froze. He then dropped to the floor, pulling the Captain with him. Dallas was more than aware that the young soldier's eyesight was keener than anyone else's in the unit so stayed quiet and waited until Jenkins was ready to explain his actions.

He didn't have to wait too long. The man pointed to the top of the wall, close to the corner of the ceiling. Despite the helpful pointer, Dallas couldn't see anything but blackness and the vague shapes of collected junk stuck on shelves that probably hadn't been moved for decades.

A small circular shadow unpeeled itself from the top of the wall and dropped onto the shelf below. His eyes had now adjusted to the change in light. Dallas could now make out a saucer-shaped object using its flexible body to undulate to the edge of the shelf. The thing moved like a damn caterpillar! It fell onto the top of an ancient TV then slid over the surface before bending over and moving down until it had reached the screen where it stopped.

"Just what in fuckery is that!" hissed Dallas.

Jenkins moved his shoulders a few inches closer to the wall. He lifted his knife arm, just as the thing on the front of the TV started to change. Its dark flesh peeled away in four quarters to reveal a dome the size of a dinner plate. To Dallas, it looked exactly like a fly's compound eye. He snatched the knife out of the other soldier's fingers, ran over to the abomination and slashed across. The blade sliced it clean in half with the lower portion slopping onto the carpet beside the TV. A rancid, hot grease odour filled the air causing Dallas to stagger back.

Jenkins gently took the knife back. "We had better shift our arses, sir. Pound to a penny says that wasn't the only one in here, whatever it was."

Dallas slowly walked back to the TV. Both pieces were now on the floor. The smell wasn't so vile now. "I think it was a camera," he muttered darkly. "A living biological camera." He crouched beside the small corpse and despite hearing Jenkins muttering 'gross' under his breath, Dallas carefully pulled the skin back around the creature's edges. His fingers brushed over something warm and sticky. He then made the mistake of pressing the tips of his forefinger and thumb together and discovered to his horror that he couldn't pull them apart!

"Captain, what's wrong, are you alright?"

With a little patience, help from his knee and his other hand, Dallas broke the hold. "Come and have a look at this, Jenkins. I think you'll find it rather interesting."

"Do I have to?" he replied, approaching anyway. "That thing smells like shit, or something that Henderson cooked." Jenkins crouched beside the Captain. "Yeah, that definitely looks like something Henderson fried up alright."

"Pass me your torch." When Jenkins dutifully handed it over, Dallas turned it on and played the beam across where the soldier first spotted this thing. What he saw only confirmed his suspicions.

"What does that look like to you, Jenkins?"

"Spider webs," he replied. "From a great big sodding spider. Christ, I wouldn't like to meet that bastard in real life."

"I think we just did." Dallas moved the beam, First to his previously stuck fingers and then back to the remains of the creature. "As mad as it sounds. I think this thing is part spider."

"Oh yeah, I mean that's totally insane. I mean how could a walking eye be part spider? It just doesn't make sense!"

"Yeah. Enough with the sarcasm." He played the light across the top of the wall again. That webbing wasn't there just for the sake of decoration. Dallas moved a little closer. He grabbed an old metal fire poker. He used the tip to tease away a section of thread and discovered grey fur underneath. "Bloody hell. I think that's a cat inside all that stuff, the poor sod," he muttered. Dallas turned to Jenkins. "You know, if you hadn't seen that thing with your super-sensitive eyes, it might have been us up there." The thought of suddenly finding that strong and sticky spider-like thread shooting out from the blackness and covering his face made him want to throw up.

"Yeah well, Captain. You can pin a medal on my chest if we survive this. In the meantime, should we not be finishing off our current mission before, you know, more insect giant eyed spider things catch up with us?"

Dallas shook his head. "I don't think we should go anywhere. In fact, I don't even believe that there is a threat in the next shop. I didn't see anything." He paused and used the time to wipe some gunk off his hands. "I mean, we only have the captain's say so and I'm beginning to doubt every word that man spews out." He leaned a little closer. "That bastard knows far more than he's letting on. You must have noticed that."

Jenkins nodded. "Hell yeah. That fucker even knew what those insect soldiers were called. What was it again? Mandtils or Mandril. Something like that. How could he know, unless he's already been briefed over what to expect?"

"You don't trust him?" Dallas knew the answer before the soldier even spoke, but he felt it needed saying. Especially considering what he was planning. Christ. Dallas couldn't believe he was even thinking of betraying a fellow officer.

"I wouldn't trust that twat as far as I could throw him. Excuse my French."

"So, you don't think I'm being suspicious but who's to say that Yates didn't know about those living spider camera things, and he wanted them to snare us so we'd be out of his hair?" Dallas passed the torch back to Jenkins. "With us out of the way, he'd only have Henderson to deal with. That wouldn't be too difficult. All the captain had to do was order the man into here to see where we'd gone and..." Dallas clicked his fingers. "That's the end of the line for all of us. We'd be sharing the fate of poor Tiddles up there."

"I don't understand why though? What the fuck have we done wrong?"

"I have no idea. I suggest we ask him before the devious bastard realises that we're wise to his game. Shine the torch over there in the corner." Harsh white light picked out the two objects he needed. Dallas grabbed his goodies. "Give me a few seconds then I want you to shoot into the wall twice. You got it?"

He nodded. Dallas spun around and ran over to a glass cabinet full of stuffed toys. He reached it at the same time that Jenkins fired. Just as he expected, a moment later, the shop door flew open. Thanks to Jenkins' torch, he saw Henderson run into the shop first. Yates followed a few seconds later.

"What the fuck are you playing at, Jenkins?" hissed Yates. "Did I not specifically stress that this was a silent op? Where the fuck is your Captain?"

Dallas sneaked up behind him and pulled the man's pistol from his holster. When Yates spun around, Dallas pointed the man's gun at his face. As Dallas had suspected the man jumped back and threw his arms into the air.

"What is this? You dare threaten another officer?"

Dallas chuckled. "And how exactly am I supposed to do that with an empty pistol?" He lowered the gun. "Wait, that reminds me. I have something else for you." He reached behind his legs and pulled out a supermarket carrier bag. He gave it a little shake. "Ugly looking fucker it is, Captain. Great big eye in the middle. Do you want to hold it?" Dallas threw the bag at the other captain.

"Get it the fuck away from me!" he yelled, batting it to the side. "I don't want to be caught in its dirty thread!"

Dallas couldn't quite believe that he'd just been proven right. He looked straight at Jenkins to discover the soldier already had his gun trained on the captain's head. "Oh dear. Caught out with your own cowardly babbling. Looks like you are in a bit of a pickle, my friend."

"What the frig is going on here?" Henderson looked like he wasn't sure who to aim his gun at.

"That man is guilty of murder."

"What nonsense. Come on, Henderson. Isn't it clear that these two have taken leave of their senses? Dallas you're making no sense."

He saw the man's gaze dart from Dallas to the contents of the carrier bag. "Henderson. This man practically killed our unit."

"That's bullshit!"

"Just one more word," growled Jenkins. "Go on. You lying, murdering sack of shit. Give me a fucking excuse to put a hole in your head."

"Davis shouldn't have died. This captain here could have killed that beetle there and then. If he had, Lovejoy would still be with us too."

"He said he was dry."

Dallas nodded. "Yeah you're right, Henderson. I seem to recall those words leaving his gob as well." Dallas raised the pistol, aimed at the bag and fired. Two sharp reports blasted through the shop. "Oh, it looks like I've just killed a lampshade."

"I said no weapons fire," said Yates, glaring at Dallas.

He aimed the pistol at the captain again. "If you don't start being a little more cooperative, there'll only be one more shot, Yates. After that." he shrugged. "Well, it won't matter to you anymore."

"Jesus, you really are a fucking idiot." Yates snatched the torch out of Jenkins' fingers. "What is wrong with you lot? Is it that hard to follow an order? Thanks to your incompetence, you have killed us all. I don't just mean us either. I mean our entire species."

"What are you babbling on about now?"

Yates moved back, not stopping until he reached the wall. "There's seven rounds left in that pistol, Captain. You had better make them count."

"Oh, I will," replied Dallas. "Trust me, though. I only need one."

Yates shone the torch into the corridor. "Bet your life on that? By the way, can you hear some clicking?"

The white light cleared away most of the shadows down there, only for several more long shadows to take their place. "Company!" shouted Dallas, at the sight of the insect solders running towards them. "Make your shots count!"

He threw himself down and managed to get off six shots before he ran out. Still, Dallas took down three of them. He rolled to the side. A moment later, an energy bolt fired from the last insect soldier melted the floor where he'd just been lying.

Henderson took out the remaining enemy with a shot to the head. Dallas got to his feet. "Jenkins, watch him!" He hurried down the corridor, stepping over the insect corpses. Despite the proliferation of alien weaponry scattered across the floor and the fact that they were all now running on empty, he gave the stuff a wide berth.

Yates warned them all against the temptation to mess with the enemy's staff-like weapons, claiming that they were 'infected' with a kind of computer intelligence which developed a bond to their owner, and if anyone else just happened to fire them, the staff acted like a betrayed mistress and acted accordingly. As all this 'info' came from the traitorous captain, Dallas should have treated it with the scorn it deserved but deep in his gut, this is one truth nugget that he did believe.

The corridor led directly into another shop. This one sold shoes. They were everywhere, apart from the facing wall. Something else now occupied that space. Dallas thought he couldn't become any more traumatised by what he'd seen during this short but violent conflict. Dallas had just been proven wrong. He stopped at the entrance, not wanting to venture further inside, not after what his eyes were showing him.

He saw dozens of box shaped structures about the size of a coffee table stacked on top of each other from floor to ceiling. Dallas guessed the boxes weren't just consigned to a single layer either. There could be hundreds there. That terrible thought alone made him avert his eyes until the slow churn in his gut settled down. These cubes were wrapped in the spider silk but not opaque enough to work out their grisly contents. Each one contained a human being, somehow compressed, stretched and distorted in order to fit the shape.

He saw the shapes of faces pressed into the silk and they were screaming. Even from where he stood, Dallas could still make out their muffled sounds. How could they still be alive?

"Oh my God!"

Dallas spun around and found the others had joined him. Jenkins held a gun against the other captain's temple while Henderson just stared at all the human-shaped cubes.

"Sorry, sir," said Jenkins. "He insisted that we brought him."

"So you can gloat?" Dallas took the gun from Jenkins, intending to shoot the bastard right there. He might have even gone through with the task if it hadn't been for the sudden change in, not only his expression, but his entire posture. The man looked broken. "Go ahead. You'll be doing me a favour."

Dallas lowered the gun. "We were supposed to die in here."

"My God. At last he gets it," replied Yates. "Of course you were supposed to die in here. Your lives were over the moment the fucking idiots at command decided we needed help. Now, thanks to your cowboy antics, you have ruined what little chance we had of containing this. You killed their guardians. Now the Mantil will know we still have the means of hurting them despite their best efforts to wipe us out."

"Sir, something's happening outside." Henderson slowly walked through the shoe shop, towards the front door. He stopped directly in front of the window. "What the fuck?"

Dallas joined him. He couldn't quite believe his eyes either. A pale blue wall of light was rising from the ground. It was surrounding the entire town! Within seconds, the light had completely enclosed them, meeting in the middle to form a gigantic half dome.

"This is what we feared. They have sealed us in and ensured nothing can enter, at least, not until the Mantil forces are ready to start their invasion." Yates turned around. "These things, these cubes are for when the huge amount of cocoons hatch. Those things are everywhere. Distributed around the town."

"What are we going to do now?"

Yates smiled at Henderson. "We die. Look above us. Did you think that their precious cargo had only one type of creature guarding them?"

Dallas lifted his gaze to the ceiling and saw the whole surface had started to ripple.

CHAPTER FOURTEEN
UNLIKELY ALLIES

Ellis had to bite her bottom lip to stop the scream from escaping, yet her action did not stop a quiet whimper leaving her mouth. Jason squeezed her hand a little tighter. She couldn't work out whether it was for reassurance or as a warning not to make any more noise. Like it even mattered. Hell, she just couldn't help herself. It wasn't even the utter terror of being found by the bastards currently hunting them which made her cry out. Ellis guessed that at least that would have given her some kind of justification. It was this resin stuff which had pushed her fear levels through the roof.

A few minutes before this area started to, as Jason would say, get a little lively, her boyfriend had finally succumbed to Lorraine's relentless questioning and told them a little more of what to expect. He explained that the Mantil and the other race had developed a kind of organic technology and they had no moral code regarding the sanctity of life. He then stopped and told Aroon that they were carnivores whereas their allies ate the green stuff. The Mantil's products were so much more insidious than anything the other race could develop. Jason explained that some of their creations were able to infect the living with anything from spores ejected from creatures blended against the wall to flying predators which live off the giant wildlife which take a fancy to any other organism that just happened to stray too close.

They heard a lot of gunfire earlier on. Jason told them that he suspected the armed forces were taking out the escaped insect wildlife. Ellis kinda knew that this wasn't some theory that he'd come up with. There really were soldiers out on the streets, wiping them out. It might have been a reason to celebrate until she remembered what he said about the engineered predators. Without their usual hosts, the only thing left to feed on were the human survivors. As disgusting and sick as that sounded, what had caused her anxiety were the heart-attack inducing images that her traitorous mind kept drip feeding her.

Jason must have heard something, so he'd told them to flatten their bodies against the resin tunnel and make no sound. Compared to all the traumatising shit she had endured, not moving and staying silent should have been a doddle. To the others it probably was but they didn't have her imagination which showed her hair-fine tendrils growing out of the resin tipped with needles which pushed into her soft flesh, or the surface stretching apart behind her head to display rows and rows of teeth, or snake-like vines unfolding from the resin, wrapping around her thighs and... at that point, Ellis gasped out loud.

Perhaps the hand squeeze did have an unexpected benefit. It did shut her mind up, at least for the moment.

Jason leaned forward, looked around the corner then breathed out a sigh of relief. "Okay, kids. Looks like it's all quiet out there," he whispered. The man looked straight at Ellis while emphasising the need to stay quiet as sound travels a distance in these tunnels. He moved forward, still holding her hand. Ellis was aware that Lorraine and Aroon took up position behind her. By the sound of it, those two had developed quite a relationship judging from their continuous whispering. Ellis wasn't sure how she felt about that. She kinda believed Aroon was hers, as stupid as that sounded. Still, at least they were able to keep each other reassured. The same certainly didn't apply to Marty. He still wasn't right. The older man took up position right at the back but if she hadn't glanced over her shoulder, she wouldn't have known. The man hadn't made a single noise since leaving the café.

Knowing that the only contact she had with the resin tunnel was through the soles of her feet reassured her too. Ellis didn't need to listen to Aroon's whispers to make her feel any better, no way. Besides, unlike Lorraine, she had Jason, her strong, seemingly indestructible soldier boy. Oh Christ. Who was she kidding? It should be obvious by now that he only used her as part of his cover story. He was just a walking, lying muscle machine, as simple as that. It's the lying that hurt her more than anything. Exactly how much of his story was true? Did he really have an uncle who now lived in Bolivia? That time he told her that he broke his leg after falling out of a tree when he was fourteen. Did that really happen? Fuck. Was Jason even his real name?

She should have dumped the goon and made a pass at Aroon. At least Ellis knew where she stood with him. For a start, it's unlikely that he'd surprise them all with the shock news that in his spare time, he killed intelligent insect super soldiers. She sensed Jason slowing down. It wasn't fucking fair. Why couldn't Jason be normal? She liked the old Jason, the big idiot who spent his spare time collecting stupid toys.

"Hey, are you okay?"

She nodded, unaware that Jason had been watching her.

"Are you sure? Cos it's either been raining in here or you've been crying."

"I'm fine." Ellis gave that oh so concerned face the best smile she could. "Just been thinking about all those poor people who lost their lives today, that's all" Fuck him and the horse he rode in on. If Jason could bullshit his way through this catastrophe then so could Ellis.

The response that Ellis received wasn't quite the one she expected.

"The ones who perished Ellis, were the lucky ones," he growled. His grip on her hand tightened. "I need you to see this. The same rules apply. No fucking noise. This time, if you do, we'll all end up in your own version of hell." He pulled her around a corner then dropped down, taking Ellis with him. "This is what we all tried to avoid," he whispered. "Go on, take a look. Don't worry. Those creatures are too concerned with their own immediate needs to care about any observers. Even so, that doesn't mean that their trainers will be as complacent."

The tunnel had taken them into the second floor of what, until yesterday, was a large shoe shop. Silk webbing and pieces of broken up cocoons covered up most of what this shop once sold. Ellis wished she could have continued looked at the stuff covering the shoes, trainers, and slippers. As horrible as that stuff was, it paled in comparison to what lay beyond her peripheral vision. The gasps of horror coming from both Lorraine and Aroon should have warned her not to look but since when did her body take any notice of her senses?

She saw humanoid insects chowing down on big boxes full of raw meat. Sure, it was pretty disgusting but it wasn't the worst abomination that her eyes had shown her today. It certainly didn't warrant the absolute look of sickness plastered upon the faces of her friends.

Her guts, and the desire to throw up and run away joined the others when Ellis spotted that two of those insect things were wearing shoes. She looked away, her gaze finally finding Jason. Those monstrous things are what came out of the cocoons?

He took a deep breath then wiped a couple of tears from his cheek. "There's a high probability that you passed most of those monstrous things every day whilst inside the market. There's also a high probability that you also walked past some of those boxes of compressed meat as well." He opened his jacket and pulled out three guns. Jason slapped them into their hands, missing Marty out. "This handgun is a Glock 17 and that is also the number of rounds inside the magazine." He then pulled out a spare magazine and showed them how to eject the old one and how to set a fresh one before handing them all two more spares.

"Just what the hell do you expect me to do with this?" demanded Lorraine. She held the gun as if it was about to explode. "We're not soldiers, Jason."

"I know that," he replied. "Neither are those creatures down there. At least, not yet. Besides, there's not much difference between that gun and the one you lost earlier on."

"You're serious about this aren't you?" said Ellis

Jason slowly nodded. "Look through the shop window and tell me what you see."

Ellis had already noticed that the sky had changed colour. It hadn't occurred to her at first that it should be dark by now. They had been in here for hours! It actually felt like days but she knew it was probably around nine. Even if it had only been a single hour since the shit hit the fan, that sky should not be the same colour as the ocean. "What the hell is that?"

"We're all trapped in here," he hissed. "That's their way of ensuring this operation of theirs stays on track. Nothing gets out and nothing gets in until they decide. At least, that's what they think." Jason pushed his way past Lorraine and Aroon then jumped off the edge and vanished into the blackness.

"What the hell is he doing?"

"How am I supposed to know what he's sodding doing, Lorraine?" She spotted a shadow moving at high speed towards a group of four insect soldiers. Ellis turned her attention to them and noticed they weren't as eager to consume the packages of meat. The other soldiers were digging into that stuff like a deer carcass torn apart by a pack of starving wolves. Their mantis-like faces were looking up to where they were hiding! One of the soldiers raised a staff-like object. It had to be a weapon.

Aroon grabbed Lorraine and pulled the woman back into the corridor. "Ellis, don't just stand there. Get back in here, out of the way. Those things are going to kill us! Ellis, I've seen what those weapons are capable of."

Aroon's urgent pleas abruptly stopped when two gunshots, coming from below, momentarily deafened Ellis. She spun around and saw one of the soldiers splayed over a meat cube. The other soldiers had scattered in all directions.

The sound of receding footsteps suggested that Jason's only back up now consisted of just her. Marty had slumped himself against the wall, seemingly oblivious to their current predicament. Oh fuck, what could she do about any of this? Ellis worked in a factory for crying out loud. She jumped and almost shot herself in the foot when a pair of hands landed on her shoulders.

"Aroon's run away, the bloody coward." Lorraine gently pulled Ellis to her knees. "Looks like it's up to the girls to rescue the hunk." She grinned. "Ellis, if we do get out of this alive, we're having a threesome, simple as." Lorraine winked, dropped onto her front and crawled closer to the edge.

If they did get through this fucking mess intact, Ellis might even go with her friend's ridiculous suggestion, if she wasn't simply having her on. Ellis joined her friend who was about to slip over the edge. More than likely, Lorraine was just winding her up. She followed her over and landed on a collection of foam-filled seats. Her friend pulled her off, brought a single finger to her lips and motioned Ellis to follow her.

She looked back to where they'd come. Three insect soldiers were already on the next level. As to how they had gotten up there so quickly was answered when Ellis looked to the left and saw another four of them climbing the wall like flies. "You have got to be fucking kidding me," she muttered. Ellis reached out, grabbed Lorraine's arm and pulled her back. "Wait, what about Marty? We can't leave him up there!"

Lorraine held onto her. "We don't have a choice, honey. Come on, we need to find your boyfriend."

Ellis stayed where she was, not believing that poor Marty still hadn't moved. It's like he either wasn't aware of the danger he was in or just didn't care. The soldiers were almost on top of him before the man finally reacted. Marty lifted his head off his chest and looked both ways. He tried to get up but his legs collapsed from under him. He hit the ground hard.

"Please, Ellis. Turn away. You really don't want to see what they'll do to him."

As much as Ellis wanted to, she just couldn't turn away. The soldiers reached Marty's body, stopped, gave him a cursory glance then continued their progress to the resin tunnel where they met up with the wall climbers. All seven soldiers vanished inside the tunnel.

"What just happened, Lorraine?" Marty now lay motionless. She so hoped that what she'd just witnessed wasn't a seizure. Then again, even it was, they were hardly in any position to help Marty.

"I've no idea, honey. All I know is that the man is probably in less danger than we are. Come on. We have to move. I think I see him now."

Ellis followed the woman as she slowly made her way through the empty metal aisles, all devoid of shoes. There were so many soldiers left down here. It appeared that most of them went after Aroon. Lorraine was right, she now saw Jason as well. He had taken up position behind a large cardboard display stand. There were four insect soldiers still feasting on one of those meat blocks, obviously oblivious to his proximity which made her wonder why those bastards were still alive! Did Jason think they wouldn't eventually discover him, as if, just like

Marty, he had some kind of immunity? Lorraine skidded to a halt and dropped down. Ellis followed at the sight of two more insect soldiers. They walked straight past them. She risked a peek over her shoulder.

Marty had moved! It wasn't much, the poor man had managed to return to his slumped against a wall position. It meant he wasn't dead though. That had to account for a win for the home team?

"Why are they still hanging around?" hissed Lorraine.

Ellis shrugged, like she had the answer for that. She couldn't even figure out how Marty had survived his encounter. Could it have something to do with Jason not giving the man one of these guns? Ellis recalled watching a movie back when she was a kid. Some rubbish about this alien hunter only killing people holding weapons. Ellis sighed. Like it really mattered.

"At last!" Lorraine waited for the soldiers to turn the next corner before running to the next aisle. She turned around. "Come on!" she whispered urgently.

Ellis ran after her.

"Christ, woman. You picked a dumb time to start daydreaming," whispered Lorraine. "You looked like you were on another planet."

"Another town would suit me right about now." She lifted her head a little higher. There didn't appear to be any more soldiers standing between them and Jason but it wouldn't stay this quiet for long. Something must have spooked the insect soldiers. They were becoming a little agitated. Ellis hoped to God that those things hadn't already worked out that they had company. She picked up a stray slipper, pulled out the insole and twisted it before tying it in a knot.

"What are you doing now?"

"Making sure we're not cut down by friendly fire," she replied. It struck her as unreal that Jason still hadn't spotted them. That soon changed when the insole gently bounced off his back. The man spun around, saw the two women and ushered them over. "As easy as that." Ellis grinned at Lorraine then pulled her across the gap.

Ellis opened her mouth to ask the big hunk what he was playing at, only for Jason to hush her. He moved to the side and pulled Ellis to the front. "The cavalry has arrived," he whispered.

Her first sighting of their allied race made her go cold and she had no idea why. There were just three of them, they didn't look all that different to the insect warriors currently hunting them. The same physical configuration except that their edges weren't so sharp. Oh, and their colourings were more muted. Their subtle differences reminded Ellis of the contrast between a bee and a wasp.

The new guys were tooled up with a much shorter version of the enemy staff weapon. They also carried a highly polished dinner plate sized object in their other appendage. Could that be a shield? Ellis turned her head towards the other group of insects at the other end of the room. They had returned to the meat cubes and were finishing off the wet remains. The new set of insects suddenly broke cover. Two fired their weapons which melted the heads of two enemy insects. The sole survivor threw itself behind the cube but the improvised cover had no effect in keeping it safe from harm. The allied insects fired again. The stream of energy turned the mass of meat into superheated steam which boiled the survivor alive.

"These new guys don't mess about," muttered Lorraine. "Glad they're on our side."

Jason stood up. "It might be best if you two stay here. They really hate confrontation and tend to get a bit twitchy. We don't want any accidents. Won't be a mo. I promise."

He scrambled past Ellis, not giving her the chance to resent him denying her the chance to 'have a word' to the creatures who were partly responsible for this fuck up. Not that she intended to take the slightest bit of notice of Jason's advice. "You're not the boss of me," she said under her breath.

Lorraine grabbed her arm. "Didn't you hear what he said?"

"Sure, I heard every word. Come on, let's go say hello to a bunch of talking termites." The false bravado melted away as soon as the group of insects noticed Jason was not alone. The change in their posture startled the hell out of her but not as much as when two of them raised their weapons.

Ellis had no desire to allow a bunch of over-sized ants turn her into a puddle of goo. She placed her hands on her hips. "Just what the hell do you think you're playing at? We're supposed to be on your side, for crying out loud. What, you can't tell the difference between human and insect now?"

Lorraine clung to her side. Ellis felt the poor woman shaking like a leaf. She was just as terrified, just hoping that her boisterous front would actually work, if not, there was always her knight in shining armour there to calm down their twitchy fingers.

It did seem to work. The tallest of the group lowered its weapon and the others followed suit. It then suddenly jumped forward, stopping less than an inch from her face. It took every ounce of her willpower not to turn on her heels and run away. The same didn't apply to Lorraine. If Ellis hadn't grabbed her, the woman could well have been on the other side of town by now.

"We all apologise as is our type," it replied. The Deltin raised its gun arm, expertly spun the weapon and casually dropped it into Ellis's hand. "A gift. Much happiness shows we, although genetically dissimilar, shared characteristics which our descendants will celebrate."

She had absolutely no idea how to respond to that. The weapon felt so weird. Warm and pliant. It took a great deal of restraint not to throw it back at the insect. Ellis cocked her head to the side, trying to figure out exactly what to do as well as trying to figure what it had just said to her. Thankfully, Jason intervened.

"We are grateful for your acknowledgement of our shared if not genetics, but thought rooms in one dwelling. However, we do still share goals which, not yet clear, may, in time, overlap. Perhaps my friends require a sample of threat provisioning, instilled by the Mantil? Perhaps, with haste and with the lines leading to outcome?"

"Confirmation of allegiance solidified with stem rod's approval. Much relief shown by fellow companions and equipment. Jason, forgive our tentativeness regarding fellow soft-flesh. Now, agree upon haste of news. Our species has reached zenith. Eyes do not lie, sustainability impossible without intervention but stock is poor so we die."

Jason took the insect's claw. "I'm sorry to hear that, Zaratous. Don't give up just yet, my friend. I don't believe that you and your six soldiers are the last of your race. There must be more of you somewhere."

Ellis got the feeling that Jason's speech was for her benefit.

"Mantil troops already gather. They sense victory. As they are wont, only now, the enemy no longer reliant upon in-built arrogance. A baseless manoeuvre at best, but needed to suit their demands on the populace. Significant developments have proven us also relying upon in-built arrogance. For which we can only apologise, Jason. Their conversion not anticipated complete success. Cannot allow them to leave. We shall help you destroy them all."

The giant insect hung its head. Ellis could only guess that this was the creature's way of displaying shame. "Wait. How can they escape? According to Jason, we're all stuck inside this giant energy dome. Those things aren't leaving. Besides, we're not soldiers. What chance do we have against all that lot?""

"Options with one choice not needed here, soft flesh," it replied. "Their energy dome. The Mantil's plan is no longer restricted. Not soldier but seeders. They'll spread their core far once the barrier is dropped."

She needed no translation for that! Ellis couldn't believe what she was hearing. "You expect us to murder our own kind? There must be some way to cure these poor people."

The insect hung its head even lower. "The seed given form cannot revert. Mantil expect and safeguard against the obvious." It lifted its head. "You three are all there is left inside the dome."

"We should have brought the fight to them," growled Jason. "A few high-ex detonations inside their site would have made them think twice about picking a fight with us."

"Help is required and gratefully given. The hatched are dangerous but still learning. We shall remove the threat." The insects moved as one. They turned once reaching the far wall then vanished.

"Come on then," muttered Jason. "Let's get this over with."

CHAPTER FIFTEEN

He had decided not to allow these sensory anomalies to get on his tits too much. Andrew guessed that whatever the fuck he was currently seeing was what that geek described as projection. Right now, he kinda preferred the last walking hallucination of watching that sad bastard try to beat that high score as opposed to wandering through what resembled a medieval market place full of human insect hybrids.

It could be worse, a lot worse. At least none of these biological fuck ups were trying to murder him. In fact, quite the opposite. Most of them looked uneasy in his presence. Hell, a couple of them even hid under the trader tables when he passed.

"Okay, staff. I know you're just dying to start gobbing off. Fine. You can talk, I don't mind. Just none of the weird perv stuff like before. That's proper creepy."

He had no choice a while back to threaten the weapon with being snapped in half if it didn't shut its trap. The stuff it was saying was seriously freezing him out, but what made Andrew snap in the end was the simple fact that the damn thing was turning him on. How that could even happen while in the midst of the scariest and strangest situation he'd ever been in was beyond him but he couldn't deny it was happening.

[I don't see why I should tell you anything,] it pouted. [Not if you're going to continue being really mean to me.]

"Christ on a bike. Now you're trying to guilt trip me. You know, my ex played that game almost every day of our shit marriage and I'll tell you something for nothing. Didn't get her anywhere." Andrew stopped beside a stall full of fruit, at least, that's what he assumed it to be. "Come on, spill the beans. Behind that façade, I know you want to."

The staff weapon sighed loudly. [Well, maybe just this once, but only because I find your silky voice incredibly sexy. You are right. This is another projection. Only difference with this one you are in now is that this is an amalgam. A fusion of thousands of projected thoughts. What you see is your poor human mind struggling to make sense of all their jumbled up visions, pasted over the real world.]

The voice now sounded like his old history teacher. The only teacher in his high school that Andrew was actually afraid of. Was it doing this on purpose? Andrew watched two of those hybrid things right at the edge of the market. They were looking in his direction as well as pointing. Something told him that his presence here was causing more than just a minor disruption. Another hybrid distracted him, knocking into his shoulder then apologising before running off.

"I don't understand why they seem to be so afraid of me. Don't get me wrong. Them running away is far better than them shooting bolts of green lightning at me. I guess you know the reason too huh?"

[It's me,] it whispered. [It doesn't matter how well a Mantil can project, the weapons of the Order always stay visible. And only soldiers are permitted to carry weapons, naturally, the locals will be a little uneasy in your presence.]

"Oh yeah. You're insects and you're all really big with the hierarchy thing with your queen bees, worker ants and what have you."

[A bit of a generalised and stereotypical reply but why should I expect any different from a soft flesh?]

"You call us Soft Flesh?!" He snapped his mouth shut. "Sorry. Forget I said that. Go on, continue what you were going to say." The attention they were getting started to make him more than a little uneasy. Andrew hurried through the last of the market stalls and out of the enclosed building. He threaded his way through narrow alleys, heading nowhere in particular, he just followed the routes where there appeared to be fewer signs of life.

[I suppose back when we were just primal intelligences, basking in the knowledge that we were the first ever terrestrial species to achieve sentience, we did cling to the old ways, of the fixed hierarchy. Why not? It worked for countless aeons, there was no need to change.]

"That explains quite a lot," he muttered.

[No, it doesn't, Andrew. You do not understand. Our species did change. We threw off the shackles which bonded most of our society into a lifetime of servitude. Okay, so maybe the process wasn't as flowery as that and took thousands of years, a lot of sacrifice as well as huge advancements in genetics, but we did once achieve our goal of a peaceful society where every individual was free to do as they desired. But it did happen.]

He finally found an area empty of people. Andrew stopped walking. He found a round boulder which came up to his thighs and sat down on it. "So what went wrong? I'm guessing something did happen which put a spanner in the works."

[The Mantil discovered that they were not the only sentient form of insect life living within the planet's core. First contact didn't really go well. I won't bore you with the details here, Andrew. Let's just say that there were deaths on both sides and, as you can imagine, both sides blamed each other and a war started. A war that we have been fighting ever since. It's why our species reverted to the old ways of strict hierarchy. It was the only way to survive.]

"Wait on, is that it? Why can you bore me with the details? I want to know."

[I can't because a squad of Mantil troopers have become aware of our existence. They are heading our way as we speak.]

Andrew heard their footsteps moments before the soldiers shuffled into view. Seven Mantil warriors, larger than any he had encountered before, ran towards his position. He fell off the stone, and managed to scramble to his feet. Andrew managed to get a metre away from the large stone before he felt hard claws brush over the top of his head, and then...

His eyes were closed. Andrew didn't remember shutting them. He couldn't remember a lot of things, the most prominent that demanded an answer was where the fuck was he now? Andrew kept his eyes closed for a moment longer, just until his head stopped spinning. Keeping his eyes shut tight sounded like the dumbest fucking idea on the planet considering just a moment ago half a dozen armour-plated giant insects were after his head but those vile smelling bastards had gone. The fact their stink no longer assaulted his nose told him that much.

He opened one eye and moaned softly. Just the one eye was enough to show Andrew where he was. "No, no fucking way. This has to be another one of those projections." Andrew opened both eyes and brushed his fingers across the rough bed sheet covering the top bunk bed. It felt real enough. Even so, since when did that mean anything? Andrew nodded to himself. It had to be a projection. There's no way that he could somehow find himself back in his old cell otherwise.

Andrew climbed down, walked over to the cell door, grabbed the window bars and pulled. The door swung inwards. He peered out onto the balcony. The place felt deserted. Andrew resisted the urge to start shouting. "That's not very professional," he muttered. "The screws would never leave my cell unlocked." He grinned to himself. "Not after the last time."

What sort of game were they playing at? More to the point, did he really want to play? Not wise considering he didn't know the rules, if there were any. Andrew wandered back inside, leaving the door open. He scanned the interior, looking for anything that might help to tell him what all this was about. He'd already clocked that the staff wasn't in here, like the bastards were going to be daft enough to leave that thing lying about.

Crap, he was missing that silky seductive voice already. How weird was that. In a strange way, her voice had helped to keep his emotions kinda level. Not exactly chilled out, that wasn't going to happen, but calm enough to stop him from losing his rag every ten minutes.

There was nothing else that might help him on his unknown quest, not that Andrew really expected to find anything. Useful items like a shotgun, a teleport bracelet or the keys to a motorbike were not the usual things to find inside a prison cell. He closed his eyes and counted to three. Upon opening them, he found the room hadn't reverted. Andrew wasn't all together sure he would have wanted to go back to outside that marketplace, not with the soldiers getting ready to stove his head in.

A beach would have been nice though. Andrew shrugged to himself, grabbed the cell door and walked out onto the balcony...and found himself back in that rented hotel room. "Okay," he yelled. "Now you're taking the piss!"

The room didn't look any different to when they were last here. The playing cards hadn't been put away. The two coffee cups were by the side of the chairs and Nelson's baccy tin was still on the upturned crate. "The old bastard was looking for that," he murmured. Andrew approached the table, picked up the cards and started shuffling them while trying to figure out what all this bullshit meant.

Andrew turned the cards over. "Oh yeah, fucking hilarious. My sides are splitting." Every card showed a picture of his face wearing a joker's hat. Andrew dropped the cards.

He walked over to the window, not totally sure what to expect. Andrew had the feeling that whatever all this was leading up to, the answer lay beyond that glass. How he knew this was beyond him, it just felt right.

The view showed the centre of town, but this was no place he recognised, at least not at first. Hundreds of skyscraper sized structures disappeared into the dark, grey clouds. Each one identical and composed of the same pale blue honeycomb material. "Bloody hell," he said. Andrew pressed his face against the cold glass and squinted. The honeycomb covered the original buildings! Through the gaps, he could make out brickwork, shopfront displays as well as bits of signage.

There were insects everywhere. The giant things, the bastards that took out most of the population made up the majority but every now and then, he saw bipedal insects. He guessed they were the Mantil invaders but it was hard to tell at this distance.

This was what the future held for this planet if those bastards were not stopped right here. He turned away and saw whoever was fucking with his mind had done it again.

The room had stayed the same but there were differences. The playing cards were back on the table, he also saw he was no longer alone. Nelson sat in his chair, giving him the evils. The old man picked up his cup, found it empty and dropped it. The cup hit one of the chair legs and the handle snapped off.

"You're dead."

Nelson's expression changed. The scowl fell away and a nasty grin took its place. "Yeah, thanks for that, you tosser. Still, I shouldn't complain too much, I guess. Where I am now is a shit load better than what my life used to be like."

"What do you want?"

He leaned forward. "What do I want? I want to smash your head against the wall over and over until your mashed brains leak out of your ears." He shrugged. "We don't always get what we want though, do we? It's what they want, Andrew. I'm just the messenger."

"Right, that's a relief. So they don't want to kill me?"

Nelson laughed. "Oh, you're a funny guy. Course they want you dead, you daft fucker."

"Oh."

The old man got out of the chair. "Man, don't look so fucking down in the dumps. It's only your body that dies." He tapped the side of his head. "They'll keep what's up here going. They were able to sort me out. I mean, if they can stitch me up after what you did to me, they'll have no problem processing you." Nelson's left arm snapped out. His fingers tightened around Andrew's wrist. "You're special to the Mantil. They want you so bad. Best go quietly. Seriously, you really don't want to make a fuss."

Andrew ripped his arm back. Gave the old man the sweetest smile he could muster then pushed him back into the chair. "Thanks, but I think I'll decline."

"That's the wrong answer. You are something special, man. You can operate their technology. That shouldn't be able to happen! Andrew, I'm begging you here. Let them absorb your consciousness. Help the Mantil move up to the next level."

"Man, you really have lost it. Watch my lips, Nelson. Go fuck yourself." He made a beeline for the open door, fully aware that the old man had left the chair and was coming after him. He ran through and found himself back in the prison cell.

"Come on, for fuck sake. Can I not have a break?"

It took him a few seconds to realise that this cell wasn't the same as the one he left earlier. He also realised that whoever was doing this to him certainly wasn't in any mood to give him any kind of break. The thing on the top bunk proved that.

Andrew slowly backed away. He didn't leave the cell, not yet. Christ knows where he'd end up if he went through that door. A place worse than this? Unlikely but still possible, although he wasn't sure how it could get any worse. The thing slivered along the top of the bed. A pair of segmented, dark green appendages curled around the metal bar and a distorted Mantil head lifted from the cover. A pair of black compound eyes fixed him to the spot. They drilled right through to his inner core. Whatever defiance he had left just melted like hot wax. Andrew wanted to scream, to shriek out and beg this vile creature to pull its cold, mental tendrils out of his mind. He knew that this thing, this beast stripping out every part of his being piece by piece was the Mantil's main leader. The queen, the creature which ruled over an empire of billions.

It slid off the bed and dropped onto the floor, landing in front of him in a large wet lump.   For a brief second, its vice-like grip on his mind relaxed, enabling Andrew to realise that this monster wasn't all that different from the Mantil soldiers, only a third taller and its innards weren't protected by an armoured exo-skeleton.

Andrew tried to flee but his shaking body betrayed him. He turned around and fell onto his face. That thing had already drained every ounce of physical and mental strength from him, leaving Andrew as weak as a baby.

One of its appendages curled around his neck and dragged him onto his feet. It turned him to face its eyes again and that mental stranglehold returned with vengeance. The bastard knew that Andrew didn't have a hope of escaping. All it had to do was to prise open the last door and it would be all over for him. All that would remain of Andrew would be a hollowed out, dried husk.

It easily brushed away what little defences he'd managed to erect and tunnelled even deeper inside, eager to uncover what secrets Andrew kept.

A bright, dazzling white light erupted and he knew it was all over. In a few moments, the being known as Andrew would simply cease to exist.

[Get your stinking paws out of his head, you dirty freak! Andrew, come on, darling. You need to fight the bastard. Focus.]

"Focus? Focus on what?" The pain the thing originally inflicted on him came back even worse. "Focus on what?" he repeated. Andrew wanted it to stop. He had already resigned himself to whatever fate that thing had lined up for him.

[It's just another projection, Andrew. You have to influence the outcome. You have the same built in abilities as every Mantil. Use it,

Andrew, bring me forward. Pull the staff weapon into this fucking projection, Andrew. Hurry, before it regains control!]

The notion sounded so simple. All he had to do was imagine it by his knees and it would appear.   That's all it would take but to accomplish even that, Andrew had to wrestle some control back from the intruder. It would only be a small amount but even that proved to be as slippery as the creature itself: those segmented appendages had him firmly tethered. Nothing Andrew tried shifted them.

"I can't do it!"

[Then you're going to die here. Is that what you really want, my precious? I don't think you do.]

A deep grinding sound rumbled through his mind. That thing was laughing at him. The bastard thought it had won! "Not yet you haven't," he said through gritted teeth Andrew stopped trying to fight it. Instead, he opened up his mind much to the wailing cry coming from the voice of the staff weapon. The creature tasted victory and dived through. When it did, it left its own mind momentarily unguarded.   Andrew seized his chance and pushed with all his might.

The creature roared in both shock and fury. Obviously not understanding how such a primitive creature could possibly penetrate the mind of such a powerful and ancient being. He had just seconds to do what he intended before this mind swatted him into oblivion.

Andrew used the creature's own mind to imagine the staff weapon beside him. He snapped open his eyes and there it was, he couldn't remember ever seeing anything so beautiful in his life. Andrew snapped it open and rolled out of harm's way.

"Eat this, you fucking bastard!" he growled. Andrew squeezed the base, grinning wider that he'd ever grinned when a blast of super-heated energised particles literally turned the creature into a puddle of smoking gloop.

Andrew fell to his knees. He felt so tired, drained of energy and of will. He looked at the stinking puddle of black goo slowly flowing towards a drain in the corner of the cell. "Is that it then, is it dead?"

[Honey. What part of it's only a projection do you not understand? It isn't dead. You can't kill the Mantil Queen so easily. All you have done is pissed her off but you have managed to buy yourself enough time to get out of here. Come on, my darling. You need to stand up.]

That took some effort but after a few moments, and help from the corner of the bunk bed, Andrew got back on his feet. He found the door had now transformed into an archway. "Where does that go?"

[Does it matter? As long as it takes you out of here and away from the clutches of that bastard insect queen who wanted to absorb you. Andrew, don't just look at it. Go through, let's get out of here!]

Andrew didn't need telling twice. He held the staff weapon tight, walked into the swirling mass of blue light and vanished.

CHAPTER SIXTEEN

Ellis grabbed Lorraine's arm and pulled her back from the edge.

"Jesus!!" she gasped. "Nice catch."

"Are you okay?"

The older woman nodded. "Yeah, I think so. Just a bit shaken. That resin stuff just collapsed from under my feet!"

She steadied Lorraine then squeezed past the woman. Ellis saw where Lorraine had almost fallen, crouched and ran her fingers over the surface. The resin fell away at her touch.

"Be careful!"

"Don't worry," Ellis replied. "I think we've arrived." She looked over her shoulder and found three pairs of eyes staring back at her.

"Where are we?" asked Jason.

The dissolved resin fell about three feet and splattered onto a very familiar stone surface. She lay down and carefully pushed her head through the hole. "You've got to be having a laugh," said Ellis under her breath.

"Are you going to answer me?" asked Jason.

She flipped onto her back and sat up. "We're back at the market. Only," she shrugged. "Only it's changed. A lot." Ellis got to her feet. "It's a bit of a drop but not that bad."

"Wait a minute," said Lorraine "What do you mean that it's changed?"

Ellis laughed. The noise felt so weird to her. "Let's just say the chances of grabbing a burger or picking up a new pair of jeans is pretty much zero now." She turned around and lowered herself onto the market floor. Ellis bent low and shuffled forward until she was clear of the remains of the resin tunnel before standing up.

"Christ. What the hell have those things been doing in here?"

Ellis wished she could answer Lorraine's question. She'd like to know too. Some kind of light blue hexagonal scaffolding now covered the outsides of every stall. Ellis reached out with her arm then drew it back, not daring to touch it, in case the stuff jumped onto her bare flesh. It was alive, the stuff had grown over the wood. The tiles at each base were cracked and pushed up to allow the intruding stuff to take hold. Was that stuff under the ground as well? Ellis resisted the urge to bang her head against the honeycomb for asking such a dumb question. Of course it was underground.   It's where all this stuff as well as the insects came from. Christ. If this was happening in here, then what did the town look like now? Their homes were being terraformed before their very eyes and there was absolutely nothing they could do about it. Could this situation possibly get any worse?

A sharp scream split through the air. She spun around. Lorraine had gone as white as a sheet. Her gaze was fixed on the honeycomb. "It's okay, honey. I don't think it's harmful. I wouldn't advise touching it though. You know, just in case."

She slowly turned her head to face Ellis. "What?" She scrunched up her face. "I wasn't looking to that, Ellis. Have you seen inside? Oh God. I bet all the stalls are the same!"

"They are," replied Jason.

He had already peered into a stall which used to sell comics. Her boyfriend was now kicking away some of the encrusted blue stuff growing up a nail bar. Three weeks ago, she had made an appointment in there. Ellis wanted to surprise Jason with a new look. She planned to have her nails done, buy a new outfit as well as sorting out her messy hair. As plans went, it was perfect. That is until the factory called her in for three extra shifts during that week.

"This one is full of them as well." Jason spun around. His gaze caught something behind the others. "Fuck, this is not good." He bent down, ran over to Ellis, grabbed the girl's wrist and pulled her down. He gestured to Lorraine and Marty. "Hide!" he hissed. "We've got company!"

She smelled them before their enemy became visible. A kind of wet, rotting seaweed stink. Two newly-hatched Mantil strode past their hiding place, followed by a bright red beetle. That thing was where the smell was coming from. Christ, it really did stink. Ellis risked discovery by raising her arm and holding her nose shut with her fingers.

The beetle stopped at the point where Jason had kicked in the honeycomb. It spun around and some sort of sticky, white fluid burst from its abdomen. The stuff spread over the broken pieces and brought the structure back to how it originally looked.

It turned around and tidied up a few stray threads before scurrying off towards the two Mantil. This was just unreal. How could they possibly fight this? "Why are we even bothering?" she said. Jason turned his head and asked her to be quiet. "Be quiet? What's the point? Admit it. We're all going to die down here and you know what is the saddest part about that, Jason? Nobody will even know that we all tried our fucking hardest to stop this."

Jason turned and tried to wrap his arms around her. She pushed him away. "You can't give up, Ellis. It's not over yet. We still have a chance.

You just need to have faith."

Ellis laughed. "Have faith? Oh, please, just fuck off, Jason. Admit it. We might as well lie back and let them take us."

"Stop that bullshit," he growled. "Just fucking stop it, Ellis. We're not finished yet."

Ellis stood up, no longer caring if the beetle or the two Mantils saw or heard her. All that mattered to her right now was to prove how wrong Jason was. "You want to know how fucked we are?" She booted the honeycomb covering the nail bar as hard as she could, gaining a little bit of satisfaction when a narrow crack appeared across two of the beams.

"Stop it!" cried Lorraine. "You'll bring that beetle back."

"I think that's what she's trying to do," said Marty.

Ellis kicked it again and again, not stopping until four of the beams had crumbled away. The bunched up cocoons were clearly visible through the gap she'd made. Jason was right. They really had packed them inside. She felt a pair of hands settle on her shoulders and assumed it was Jason getting ready to ask her if she was alright. It surprised her a little to find the hands belonged to Marty.

"You are right, you know," he said. The older man kept his voice low enough so only she could hear his words. "I knew it back when I saw just how many of those things there were back when we were in the pub. As soon as I saw how easily they'd overrun the place, I knew we were all living on borrowed time." He pulled a kitchen knife out from his belt. "Just say the word and I'll do you right now. Don't worry. It's pretty sharp so it won't cause too much pain. One deep cut across the side of the neck and you'll probably be dead before your body hits the floor."

Ellis tried to back away, only for Marty to grab her wrist tight.

"I see you're suddenly a little frightened? Don't be, my precious. I'll be dead soon after once I cut you, Ellis. Do you think Jason will allow me to live after I kill you?" He grinned. "Not a chance. He'll put a bullet through my brain in a second!"

What the fuck was wrong with him? Oh Christ, she didn't want to die anymore, certainty not by the hands of the crazed psycho. Where did that ultra sweet middle-aged perfectly harmless man go to? The one who she always shared her problems with? The one who had, on many occasions managed to put her back on the straight and narrow?

That question remained unanswered thanks to the cocoon hanging behind Marty shifting to the side. The middle-aged man seemed unaware of the movement, his attention was fixed on the tip of the knife he held. The surface about a quarter of the way down its length bulged out. Five points, arranged in a circular pattern pushed even further out.

That thing in there was trying to get out! The stuff continued to stretch like some giant brown balloon. Marty finally realised that something was amiss when the skin started to split. An unformed limb, partly human but covered in pieces of cartilage-like shell burst through one of the holes.

Marty suddenly released her wrist. He swapped the knife into his other arm then spun it in a high arc. The blade sliced across the cocoon, cutting deep. Ellis stumbled back and fell into Lorraine's arms. She watched in utter horror and revulsion as thick, brown fluid spattered across Marty's face as he continued to stab and slash at the thing inside that chrysalis.

"Marty. Come on, man," said Jason. "I think it's dead now."

The man didn't appear to hear, he continued to mutilate the thing. Ellis tried desperately not to throw up. She knew that if that cocoon hadn't started to move when it did, he would have done that to her. He only stopped when another of the cocoons started to move. He made a beeline for it only for Jason to push past her and Lorraine. He smacked the knife out of Marty's hand then grabbed the back of his collar and wrenched him out of the market stall. "Enough, I said. For crying out loud."

Jason pulled out his gun, aimed at the top of the cocoon and put one bullet into it. The cocoon immediately ceased its movements. He walked over to where the knife went, picked it up then hurried to Marty and helped him onto his feet. "Seriously, man. A single stab to the face ought to do it. No need to go full postal on them." He pushed the knife handle into Marty's palm. "Come on, no point in hanging about." He raised the gun and aimed at another cocoon.

"What are you doing, Jason? We can't kill them all in cold blood."

"Yes we can," replied Marty. "I'm going to enjoy it too. It's payback time."

What was wrong with him? A moment ago, he said it was pointless to fight back, and now? Her head was starting to hurt.

"You heard what our allies said. We have to kill them. They're carriers. When they get out of here, they'll spread this mutation across the planet."

"It just feels so wrong. It feels like murder. There has to be another way."

"I'm sorry, honey." Lorraine took out her own pistol. "Your boyfriend is right. We have to do this. There really is no other choice." She aimed her gun at another cocoon inside the nail bar and fired off two shots.

"This is madness!" cried Ellis. She felt utterly alone. Both Lorraine and Jason were now finishing off the ones in the nail bar while Marty had gone into another market stall. There were no gunshots coming from that direction so she guessed the psycho had gone back to using his knife again.

Ellis caught movement in the corner of her eye. Oh God, those things were coming back! "We have to get out of here." They couldn't hear her. They were making too much noise. She reached inside the nail bar and frantically tapped Lorraine on her shoulder. The woman just brushed her hand away and moved further inside. What was wrong with the stupid woman? Ellis had no choice but to get away and hope they'd realise the danger before it was too late. She threw herself to the left, hoping that none of the invaders had spotted her, that they were too focussed on the commotion going off in the nail bar to notice her. Ellis moaned softly at the sight of three Mantil soldiers peeling away from the main group. She knew they were coming after her!

Her only hope was to lose them within this labyrinth and pray that those things would lose interest and leave her alone. Ellis raced away from her friends. She said a silent prayer for them too, hoping that they'd realise the danger they were in and kill those bastards before they ran out of bullets.

It took her just a few seconds of dashing left and right through this weird petrified alien-like forest of hexagonal structures to lose both her and those pursuers. She could still hear them, scuttling up and down the aisles. She carried on going, hoping to double back and join up with the others without getting caught. Since the appearance of this new batch of insects, Ellis hadn't heard any more gunfire. She couldn't work out whether that was a good or bad thing. Oh hell, Ellis had managed to get herself lost. Nothing looked remotely recognisable. This coral-like stuff had continued to grow and thicken, pushing away and destroying more of the original stalls, making it almost impossible for Ellis to work out the location. Her only hope was to reach the end wall and take it from there.

Ellis put on a burst of speed, eager to reach the wall. She knew now that separating from the others was a crap idea. Even if they had refused to listen, those people were still her friends and they deserved better than for her to run out on them. Ellis slowed down then skidded to a stop. She crouched beside one of the structures, convinced that her pursuers were down the next aisle. She heard footsteps, getting louder and louder. They were almost on top of her!

Three Mantil warriors passed within inches of her fingers. If just one of them happened to look down then she knew the game was up. One of them decided to stop. She had to whip her hand back so it wouldn't stand on her. Ellis's heart sped up. The loud beating sounded thunderous and the longer they stayed the more certain she became that at any moment one of those giant insect things would hear it too.

They began to converse in some strange language that seemed to be composed more of clicks and whistles than of actual words. After another few seconds one of them actually shifted away. Were they going? Ellis hoped so. Cramp had begun to set in. The lead Mantil made another series of clicky whistles before running back the way it came. Finally, they were leaving! Ellis sat up and arched her back. As she twisted her head, something inside the stall, just beyond the honeycomb framework, moved. A sharp cry bellowed out from within. The two remaining Mantil heard it too and turned around. They saw her crouching beside the structure, let loose another barrage of clicks, raised their staff weapons and aimed them directly at her face.

She was dead. Those things couldn't possibly miss at that distance. Ellis closed her eyes. So much for escaping death from Marty. She'd just delayed the inevitable. There was another series of clicks then the sound of one of their weapons firing and yet Ellis was still alive. How could they possibly miss? She snapped open her eyes and found one of the Mantil soldiers lying dead at the feet of the other one. The survivor looked as confused as she was.

It wouldn't stay like that for much longer. Ellis needed to get the fuck away from it before the damn thing decided to blame her for its mate's mysterious demise. She got on all fours and scurried forward. The remaining Mantil soldier roared. She heard it pick up its weapon. Ellis spun around. "Please!" she cried. "Don't blame me. I didn't..."

A stream of brilliant white heat burst out from inside the market stall and engulfed the soldier. She watched in horror as the thing literally melted like a blowtorched candle. Ellis slowly sat up and dared herself to look through the honeycomb lattice to see who had rescued her.

A very human face pushed through the now charred and brittle honeycomb lattice. "Small world, ain't it, Ellis. Fancy meeting you in here."

"Andrew. Andrew Davis, is that really you?" This was so weird. How could someone she once knew at school be here? She vaguely wondered if this was a trick, some kind of hallucination. The fact that this man gripped a Mantil staff weapon gave her theory more than enough credibility.

The man threw himself through the honeycomb wall. He brushed away the black residue clinging to his clothes and bowed. "At your service," he replied once he'd straightened himself. "It's been a bit of a weird day, wouldn't you say?"

The man then turned to the left and told his staff weapon to be quiet. "Sorry about that," he said while chuckling. "She's jealous."

His eyes travelled up and down her body, lingering a little too long at her chest. Ellis turned away and bit back the perv retort. After all, this man had just managed to save her life. "Where did you just spring from?" she asked. "We were told that there were no survivors left in town."

"Oh, you know. Here and there. Mainly there but also in here. Actually, I spent a lot of time in here. It didn't look like this though." Andrew finally took his gaze off her and inspected the stuff growing over the stalls. "I know I've been away, Ellis. To places you don't even want to know. That's not important. What is crucial for all of us, is how long ago did the insects invade? Think carefully here, cos I'm kinda hoping you're going to say a few weeks ago or, even better, a couple of years."

Ellis shook her head. "Sorry. I'm not sure. Maybe a day, possibly two?"

"Oh, fuck. That's not good. So, this stuff 's grown over these stalls in literally a few hours?" He turned to the staff weapon. "Your pals don't mess about, do they"

Ellis had no time to wonder about the man's erratic behaviour before Andrew stiffened. He pushed past Ellis and pointed the staff weapon at one of the structures.

"Come on, out you get. Don't give me a reason to fucking burn you."

Jason and Lorraine slowly emerged from behind the structure. Ellis ran over to Jason and flung her arms around him. "Thank Christ for that, I thought I'd lost you."

He pulled her back, bent his head and kissed her softly. "That's not going to happen, honey." Jason kissed her again before looking over her head. "Who's he then?" Jason held out his hand. "Hello there, friend. I'm happy to see another face." His gaze settled on the staff weapon. "I'd be very interested to learn how you were able to get that to work. I thought humans weren't able to operate Mantil weaponry."

Andrew walked forward. He held out his hand as well as wearing a big smile. The smile suddenly fell away when Marty stepped out from the other side of the structure, covered in foul smelling red and brown gore, still holding his knife.

"It's okay," said Jason. "He's with us."

The new arrival brought up the staff weapon and fired a single shot.

Both Ellis and Lorraine screamed. The bolt struck Marty in the chest. The top half of his body liquidised and ran down the man's legs. The burning fluid left thick scorch trails down the fabric.

"What the fuck?" yelled Jason. He took one more look at the remains of Marty before pointing his own gun at Andrew. "What the fuck?"

Andrew fired off another shot. This one passed within inches of Jason's head and smashed into the lattice behind him, igniting the wooden shell.

"What? Are you honestly telling me that you weren't aware that your pal was infected?" He raised the staff weapon a little higher. "You're still pointing that at me. See, the thing is, I heard the firefight," said Andrew. "And I'm guessing that you're out of bullets." He grinned. "Yes, I thought so. There goes the tell-tale facial flicker, soldier boy." He fired again, igniting another stall. "I could do this all day. Unlike human guns, my gorgeous, little temptress will not run out. Now, do the right thing and drop the gun."

Jason sighed loudly before starting to lower his pistol. "Infected by the Mantil? How can you possibly know that?"

Ellis darted her gaze to the side. The fire was spreading fast. It had already started to leap from stall to stall. The cocoons inside crackled and popped as the intense heat cooked their contents.

"There's more of them!" screamed Lorraine. "Oh God, they're coming this way."

Three bright red beetles and over a dozen Mantil soldiers were heading straight for them. They were trying to escape the spreading fire. Andrew ran past her.

"Go, get out of here. I'll hold them off as best I can"

"Thank you." Ellis tried to give the man a hug only for Jason to pull her away.

"Come on, let's get the hell out of here!"

CHAPTER SEVENTEEN

The fire was spreading faster than they could run! Ellis whimpered and gritted her teeth in pain after tripping over the hexagonal lattice which had decided to grow horizontal instead of vertical. She managed to stay upright. She knew full well that falling meant certain death. Both Jason and Lorraine were far too busy looking after themselves. Not that she blamed them. After all, she was the one who left them inside the nail bar while she ran off.

In truth though, Ellis believed her running away had nothing to do with them two not looking out for her. They were just too busy trying to save their own lives. She whimpered again when a stall right next to her burst into flames. Oh God, it had already reached them; already, the tattered shirt on her back had started to smoulder.

She cried out Jason's name. They both halted, turned, grabbed an arm each and carried Ellis. "I'm so sorry," she whispered. "I didn't mean to leave you in there. I needed to say that before we die."

Jason told her to stop being silly. "That's not going to happen. Look at that!"

"Is that your friend, Ellis?"

They had reached the resin tunnel and Lorraine was right. The figure kneeling down and frantically urging them to hurry up really was Aroon! "He's still alive!"

Jason reached the tunnel first. With Lorraine's help, they lifted her up. Aroon grabbed her hand. Once she was safe, Aroon reached down and pulled Lorraine into the tunnel. Jason managed to heave himself up. He glared at Aroon. "Me and you will be having words in a minute." He glanced back. "Once we're safely away, that is."

He pulled the rest of his body into the tunnel, scrambled onto his feet and ran over to Ellis. "Come on!" he said. "Move those legs!" Jason pulled her through the tunnel. Aroon and Lorraine were right behind them.

Aroon managed to get in front. He stopped beside the first junction they reached and told them they had to go this way.

"Fine by me," replied Jason. He helped Lorraine and Ellis inside. "Are you two okay?"

Ellis nodded. "We're still alive, I guess. As for being okay?"

Lorraine took her hand. "Just focus on the alive bit, honey. That's the most important bit. The rest will come in time."

Jason smiled at Ellis. "It's been a crazy ride, that's for sure." He then turned his attention to Aroon. The soldier wrapped his fingers around his throat. "Care to explain why you, oh so conveniently, decided to fuck off and leave us all in the lurch?"

Aroon's hands slapped at Jason's arm but it had no effect.

"I don't think he can speak. You're holding him too tight," replied Ellis. She leaned closer. "Let's hear what he has to say, Jason. Then you can throttle the bastard."

Jason eased his grip ever so slightly.

"Look, I didn't run away. I know it looks like it but I didn't. You need to believe me."

Jason looked at Ellis who nodded.

"Throttle the weasel."

"Wait!" he cried. "I know a way out. I mean past that energy barrier. It isn't as impenetrable as the insects think."

Jason lowered his arm. "You better not be lying."

"Why do you think I came back? Okay, so I'll admit it. When I saw those insect soldiers coming my way, I absolutely shit myself and ran away. There. Satisfied, Mr. fucking hero of the hour? I could have left you all in here. You know that don't you? I didn't though. I returned, only for you to act all pissy because I did what most people would probably do."

Jason backed off.

"I should think so too," mumbled Aroon. "Come on then, time's wasting."

He took off down the tunnel, not giving the others any time to catch up.

"Are you going to be alright? I mean with your leg."

"I'll be fine," replied Ellis. "You stay with Aroon and make sure he doesn't try anything."

"Oh, don't you worry about that score."

"It's okay," said Lorraine. "I'll help her." She put Ellis's arm over her shoulder. "Go, Jason. For crying out loud, before you lose him."

With Lorraine's help, she managed to cover quite a lot of ground. They didn't catch up to the other two but as the tunnel only split into two sections the one time, they were able to keep going the right way. At the split, Jason had thoughtfully dropped a couple of spent rounds to indicate which direction to choose.

"I hope he is telling the truth, Ellis. I really do. I'm not sure how much of this insanity I can take."

"I can't even answer that," she replied. "I mean, I want to believe him.

Believe me, I really do, but after all the shit we've been through, my faith is shot to shit."

The pair slowed down as daylight filtered through the tunnel. Lorraine picked up the pace, apparently forgetting she was still helping an injured woman. Not that Ellis minded. Feeling the sun on her skin after spending Christ knows how much time away was a pleasure worth the pain.

They came out in front of the town's main car park. Jason and Aroon were waiting for them. Ellis kept her gaze on the heavy, grey clouds now obscuring the sun. She didn't want to look at the extensive damage caused by that hexagonal, coral-like stuff. It was worse here than the market, much worse. The pale blue lattice had already climbed up to the third floor of most of the buildings. It totally changed the appearance of her town. It wouldn't be long before the stuff covered over every human built structure in the town.

The energy dome had not shifted. Just beyond the barrier were dozens of soldiers, armoured vehicles, even a couple of tanks. Behind them was a wire fence, holding back hundreds of people. If Aroon was right then, with luck, she and her friends would be back in the company of real people real soon. If this escape tunnel went both ways, then it would give those soldiers time to strike back and give those insect bastards a bloody nose.

"We're nearly there," said Aroon. "Come on, we have to hurry. It's not safe out in the open. There's still a lot of the flying insects around. The soldiers didn't get all of them." He ran along the car park and stopped directly outside the old cinema. "Come on, don't dawdle."

Lorraine and Jason followed him. Ellis struggled to keep up. She didn't blame them being so eager to get out of this nightmare. Jason had already told her that as soon as he got back, his first task would be to lead a squad of soldiers back in here and wipe out every single one of the bastards. Lorraine just wanted to go and visit her mum.

By the time she reached the cinema, the other three had used the alleyway beside the building. That took them to the town square. She followed them, noting that unlike the rest of the town, this area was relatively untouched. She did spot the occasional piece of honeycomb lattice precariously clinging to the damp walls. Ellis guessed that perhaps the stuff wasn't too keen on growing where hundreds of late-night pub goers had been using this alleyway as a toilet for Christ knows how many decades.

Ellis stopped at the exit, her thoughts that perhaps they might have found another weapon against the insects vanished when her eyes fell upon a new structure, right in the middle of the town square.

It stood at about four levels high, shaped like a concave spike and, from what she could tell, composed entirely of the hexagonal lattice. Unlike the other stuff, this was a deep red.

Aroon and the others stood in front of it. He waved at her, and telling Ellis to hurry up.

She stayed put and shook her head. No, no way was she going anywhere near that thing. It was difficult to tell from where she stood but it appeared that Jason was having second thoughts as well.

What was she going to do? Ellis moved forward, knowing that whatever Aroon was up to, she couldn't stay here.

Her movement away from the building saved her life as three giant black beetles and a yellow mantis emerged out of the dark shop. They saw her straight away.

Ellis screamed and ran as fast as she could towards the group. Jason ran towards her. He kept shouting but she couldn't work out what he was saying. It's only when he reached Ellis and pulled her back to the tower that she saw just how close those insects were getting.

"We're not going to make it!" She tore her gaze off the advancing armada of death and looked over to Lorraine. Aroon already had the door open. Her friend was at the doorway, urging her to hurry.

"Wait, that's not right. The insects are slowing down."

Ellis heard the words but she had no intentions of staying out here. The tower might send her guts into free-fall for some inexplicable reason but what alternative did they have?

She reached the doorway. Lorraine pulled her inside then shut the door when Jason had thrown himself through. "Where's he gone?"

"There's only one direction," she replied.

"We had better hurry," said Jason. He set off down the narrow passageway.

They travelled for less than a minute before they caught up with Aroon. He stood next to another archway. The device had already been activated. Ellis moaned softly. There was no way through the energy barrier! Jason tightened his grip. He obviously felt the same way.

"Well?" said the grinning Aroon. "Don't just stand there like a trio of imbeciles. In you go. Oh, there's no point even thinking about going back the way you came. I've already remotely opened the door. Several beetles are currently examining the doorway, probably wondering if there's any food in here."

Tears ran down her eyes. He was right. What other choice did they have? "Are you ready?"

Lorraine nodded. Jason bent down and kissed her before nodding too. Ellis kept her grip on his hand then closed her eyes and stepped through.

"Oh, you have got to be joking!"

Ellis snapped her eyes open. The first sight that greeted her was her friend standing next to Aroon wearing a huge smug smile. She looked away, already aware of the ramifications.

They were in the middle of a huge auditorium. Thousands of Mantil eyes were watching them. Ellis then saw the two open cocoons "Oh no. Please. Not that!"

Lorraine grabbed her while Aroon took Jason. She tried to fight but, just like her boyfriend, their efforts had absolutely no effect.

"Lorraine. What the fuck is wrong with you? Let me go!"

"Sorry, honey," she replied. "I'm no longer Lorraine. The other human was right about Marty. He infected and changed me, back in that DIY shop." She pushed Ellis into the open cocoon and as soon as her arms and legs were inside, pale, wet webbing burst out from the cocoon 's green flesh and wrapped over the limbs, fastening her in place. Jason was still fighting Aroon, struggling and shouting. He soon stopped when more webbing wrapped over his limbs, including a thick strip curling over his mouth.

Aroon leaned inside Ellis's open cocoon, "Out of the thousands of humans in this town, who could have possibly believed that you could be one of the two survivors? If I wore a hat, I'd take it off to you."

"Let us go, Aroon!" she sobbed. "How can we be of use to you?"

Aroon giggled. "Strange choice of words there. Your little friend here said the exact phrase right after I ate his father's brain. I stood over the shivering individual back in his dad's restaurant while wondering what to do about killing the few human survivors still in the town. In a way, his words are the reason why you're in this mess, Ellis. The burning of my other infected humans and Andrew's refusal to join me had something to do with it but that's beside the point."

The lid began to close.

"Oh God. Please. I don't want to die!"

"Who said anything about dying? You two are going to help us infect and alter the rest of your species. You're obviously of good genetic stock."

The lid closed. Ellis screamed and shrieked, only stopping when freezing gelatinous fluid rapidly filled up the interior and poured down her throat.

CHAPTER EIGHTEEN
THE FINAL ACT

He didn't ask why a beautiful woman's supple fingers were massaging his thighs. His mouth stayed shut. It felt like the right thing to do. She kinda reminded him of a gentle deer. Granted, a gentle deer with long auburn hair, full sensual lips and a chest he could lose himself in.

Opening his mouth and coming out with some stupid wise crack might make her run off. Oh, those fingers really were the business. All the tension built up since this bollock-fest fell on him slowly eased away. Leaving more relaxed than he'd felt even before those bastards put him inside for his last post office job.

"Andrew, change is now inevitable, but for better or worse is now in your hands alone." The woman pulled her fingers back.

He wanted to beg for this adoring female to continue. It didn't matter that he'd just figured out who she was. All Andrew wanted right now was to feel those expert hands upon his flesh.

Is this how she used to look? Did the essence of his staff weapon once possess a human body, or was this just how she wanted him to believe she looked?

"You have allies. Ones you have already met and ones still in the shadows. You have to act now or everything will be lost!"

The woman sat up. Andrew tried to scramble backwards but his legs refused to function. The woman's shape altered. It lengthened and lost mass.

"You have got to be shitting me," he growled, when armoured sections of dark-green shell grew rapidly over the creature's body. "A Mantil."

It spoke something in an unknown tongue, then raised one of its serrated arms, then slammed it into Andrew's guts...

He sat up, screaming in agony. There was no Mantil anywhere near and his guts were intact. Andrew managed to turn his head and saw exactly why the excruciating pain threatened to make him go insane.

[It's best you don't look at it.]

"How the fuck can I not?" he screamed. "My arm is now a blackened stump!" The scorched meat reminded Andrew of burnt pork. He was going to throw up any second. The market blazed away some distance from where he lay. Andrew didn't have a clue how he had got here. Nor did he care. "The pain!" he shouted. "I can't fucking stand it any more."

[There's a chrysalis next to your undamaged arm, Andrew. I want you to sit up, stop whining like a big baby and push your fingers through the thick flesh.]

"What? What are you going on about?"

[Just fucking do it!] screamed the voice. [We're fast running out of time.]

He did as the voice commanded, even though moving just a millimetre caused the agony to treble. His fingertips touched the surface, then while holding his breath, he pushed through the outer coating.

Just for a brief moment, Andrew's mind filled with billions more voices. He sighed in ecstasy. He shook his head. The pain had gone. "What the hell just happened then?"

[We had your first connection. Don't let it bother you. Look at your arm, Andrew.]

Thick cream fluid had travelled from the hole he'd torn through the surface, down his arm, across his chest and covered the affected, blackened area. Through the glaze, he saw spots of baby pink skin peppering the burnt arm.

[Come on. Up you get. It'll heal as you move.]

"Where am I supposed to go?" He found that question didn't need an answer once Andrew had spotted the huge red tower. Several giant insects congregated around the door but they quickly scarpered when he fired a single blast of energy.

Andrew raced through the doorway and down a narrow corridor. He skidded to a stop when he saw an activated archway at the end of the passageway. "What's through there?"

[Your future,] she answered.

"Oh very helpful." Andrew counted to three then ran into the swirling blue energy vortex.

He emerged inside an arena of some sort. There were two pulsating cocoons lying on the low platform while two humans, a man and a woman, stood beside them. Thousands of Mantil stood around the platform, chanting. The noise stopped moments after they all became aware of a new arrival.

[Shoot the two cocoons,] shouted the voice.   [Please, hurry!]

Andrew took aim and fired off two shots. The human female got a little too close and the plasma energy turned her into a blazing statue.

Two wet naked figures fell onto the platform. Even from where he stood, Andrew could see the drastic changes that the enzymes inside the cocoons had caused to the bodies. They did not even resemble humans.

The remaining human clicked his fingers and one of the Mantil warriors ran over to him. The human slowly approached Andrew and as he neared, the face changed into Nelson.

"A nice entrance, Andrew," he said. "Very dramatic. A bit pointless though. They might not be fully ready for flight but give it a few more minutes to allow the changes to complete and each one will explode into billions of spores. The invasion will continue."

"Is that the Mantil Queen?"

[Yes. Put me down, Andrew. Allow me to do my part.]

He gently lowered the staff weapon then laid it on the floor.

"Very good, Andrew," said Nelson. "Now, step away and..."

The creature's words stopped in mid-sentence when Andrew's dream woman emerged from the weapon. She ran over to the Mantil warrior and whispered something into its ear. Almost immediately, the warrior pulled a small control box out of Nelson's hands, dropped it on the floor and stood on it. The energy shield blinked twice then deactivated.

"What did that achieve?" shouted Nelson. "All you have done is accelerate the invasion."

The staff weapon had reverted to its former shape. The warrior threw it over to Andrew. He caught it and aimed the business end at Nelson.

[Forget about the queen,   Andrew, shoot the two figures!]

"What?" The crowds had gone wild. They swarmed towards him

[Just do it. They are dead anyway!]

He took aim and fired. Two green balls of light rose into the air then detonated. Every Mantil in the crowd fell to the floor with the exception of the Mantil warrior.

"What have I done?" The Mantil Queen no longer resembled Andrew, it no longer resembled much of anything, apart from a lumpy green pool of spreading gunk.

The woman reappeared. She took Andrew's hand, wrapped her fingers tight around his and pulled him away from the mess. "You took the only option available and halted the genocide of two intelligent species."

"How?"

"When the liquid from the cocoon helped to heal you, for a moment, you were joined physically and mentally with the insect collective. Instead of the spires turning every human into Mantil warriors, it will now turn the humans and the Mantil into one homogeneous species. It really is the dawn of a new age."

Andrew wasn't sure how to respond to that. Instead, he turned his attention to the remaining warrior. "I don't understand why you helped."

"I was human not that long ago," it replied. "I made a lot of mistakes during my life and helping you actually felt like the right choice this time." It paused. "Or it just might be the fact that I find it impossible to say no to such a beautiful woman."

THE END

CHECK OUT OTHER GREAT HORROR NOVELS

BLACK FRIDAY
by Michael Hodges

Jared the kleptomaniac, Chike the unemployed IT guy, Patricia the shopaholic, and Jeff the meth dealer are trapped inside a Chicago supermall on Black Friday. Bridgefield Mall empties during a fire alarm, and most of the shoppers drive off into a strange mist surrounding the mall parking lot. They never return. Chike and his group try calling friends and family, but their smart phones won't work, not even Twitter. As the mist creeps closer, the mall lights flicker and surge. Bulbs shatter and spray glass into the air. Unsettling noises are heard from within the mist, as the meth dealer becomes unhinged and hunts the group within the mall. Cornered by the mist, and hunted from within, Chike and the survivors must fight for their lives while solving the mystery of what happened to Bridgefield Mall. Sometimes, a good sale just isn't worth it.

GRIMWEAVE
by Tim Curran

In the deepest, darkest jungles of Indochina, an ancient evil is waiting in a forgotten, primeval valley. It is patient, monstrous, and bloodthirsty. Perfectly adapted to its hot, steaming environment, it strikes silent and stealthy, it chosen prey: human. Now Michael Spiers, a Marine sniper, the only survivor of a previous encounter with the beast, is going after it again. Against his better judgement, he is made part of a Marine Force Recon team that will hunt it down and destroy it.

The hunters are about to become the hunted.

CHECK OUT OTHER GREAT HORROR NOVELS

DEATH CRAWLERS
by Gerry Griffiths

Worldwide, there are thought to be 8,000 species of centipede, of which, only 3,000 have been scientifically recorded. The venom of Scolopendra gigantea—the largest of the arthropod genus found in the Amazon rainforest—is so potent that it is fatal to small animals and toxic to humans. But when a cargo plane departs the Amazon region and crashes inside a national park in the United States, much larger and deadlier creatures escape the wreckage to roam wild, reproducing at an astounding rate. Entomologist, Frank Travis solicits small town sheriff Wanda Rafferty's help and together they investigate the crash site. But as a rash of gruesome deaths befalls the townsfolk of Prospect, Frank and Wanda will soon discover how vicious and cunning these new breed of predators can be. Meanwhile, Jake and Nora Carver, and another backpacking couple, are venturing up into the mountainous terrain of the park. If only they knew their fun-filled weekend is about to become a living nightmare.

THE PULLER
by Michael Hodges

Matt Kearns has two choices: fight or hide. The creature in the orchard took the rest. Three days ago, he arrived at his favorite place in the world, a remote shack in Michigan's Upper Peninsula. The plan was to mourn his father's death and figure out his life. Now he's fighting for it. An invisible creature has him trapped. Every time Matt tries to flee, he's dragged backwards by an unseen force. Alone and with no hope of rescue, Matt must escape the Puller's reach. But how do you free yourself from something you cannot see?

www.ingramcontent.com/pod-product-compliance
Lightning Source LLC
Chambersburg PA
CBHW051950170626
46808CB00007B/2550

* 9 7 8 1 9 2 5 8 4 0 6 6 7 *